SASSY & SIXTY
THE SENSATIONAL SIXTIES SQUAD

BERNICE BLOOM

DEAR READER,

Hello, and thank you so much for buying 'Sassy and Sixty'.

Welcome to a brand new series featuring Rosie Brown and the Sensational Sixties Squad!

Get ready to embark on a delightful journey with Rosie and her friends as they prove that life doesn't end at sixty—it only gets more interesting.

In this series, you'll meet a group of vibrant women who refuse to fade into the background of life. Instead, they're embracing new adventures, second chances at love, and the power of friendship.

There's the vivacious Emma, practical Lisa, artistic Julie, and sweet Catherine, Rosie navigates the challenges and joys of this new chapter in her life.

From disastrous yoga classes to impromptu cocktail parties, from facing down ex-husbands to embarking on new romances, Rosie and her friends will make you laugh, cry, and cheer them on every step of the way.

'Sassy and Sixty' is more than just a story—it's a celebration of women who refuse to be defined by their age. It's about finding yourself, cherishing friendships, and realising that it's never too late for a new beginning.

So, pour yourself a large glass of wine (or a cup of tea), get comfortable, and join Rosie and the Sensational Sixties Squad on their unforgettable adventure. I hope you enjoy reading this book as much as I enjoyed writing it.

Here's to being sassy at any age!

Bernice x

THE RELUCTANT DOG WALKER

ROSIE Brown prepared herself for battle. She breathed deeply and tried to focus. She could do this. She was in the zone and ready to go; like a boxer preparing for a world title fight.

She lifted her head, pulled back her shoulders and braced herself for what might come.

Then, it happened. The door swung open and two energetic four-year-olds ran at her, grabbing her legs and leaving sticky finger marks all over her clothes.

"Grandma, grandma, grandma," they cried, dragging her into the house.

It wasn't that she didn't love her grandchildren with every beat of her heart, but at 63 she found them quite a handful. Sometimes they would clamber all over her with such exuberance that she'd go hobbling home afterwards feeling like she'd played a rugby match.

Despite being only four years old, they seemed to have the combined strength and enthusiasm of a pair of silverback gorillas. The door opened further to reveal Mary - or, rather, a messy version of her usually put-together daughter.

Mary's hair was piled in a scruffy bun, dark circles shadowed her eyes, and was that... yes, that was food on the side of her face.

"Mum!" Mary's voice cracked with relief. "Thank God you're here. I was just about to call you."

Before Rosie could respond, a bundle of soft, golden fur launched itself at her knees.

"Elvis! No!" Mary grabbed for the excitable Cavapoo, but missed.

The dog danced around Rosie's legs, leaving muddy paw prints on her crisp linen trousers. She hadn't even got into the house yet, and she already looked homeless.

"Oh, darling," Rosie sighed, hugging her daughter. "You look..."

"Like death warmed up? Go on, mum. You might as well say it.

"Trust me, I feel worse than I look. The twins have been up all night with colds. One coughed, then the other one woke up and started crying, then the first one got upset again.

Just when they'd gone back to sleep at 3am, Elvis decided it was the perfect time for a display of his barking prowess. That woke them both up again."

"Oh lord. That sounds tough. Where's Ted?"

"He's still away on this work trip. Come in, Mum. Sorry about the mess. I haven't had a chance to... well, do anything."

Rosie stepped into the hallway, nearly tripping over a teetering stack of children's toys and books. The house, which was never the tidiest place in the world, looked like it had been hit by a tornado.

In the living room, evidence of the twins' presence was everywhere. Stuffed animals formed a protective perimeter around a play area, surrounded by sippy cups, colouring books, and what appeared to be the entire contents of Mary's wardrobe.

Mary made a beeline for the sofa, where the children were now huddled under a blanket watching cartoons.

"Grandma Rosie come and watch this. Come and see…"

Rosie's heart melted at the sight of her grandchildren. She loved them when they were all cuddled up on the sofa like that, being sweet. She found it much harder when they were jumping all over her.

She was so proud of her daughter and how she coped with two children, especially since they had endured such a difficult start in life. Her beautiful granddaughter, Daisy, had been kidnapped for the first few months of her life, thanks to a horrible nurse. Now they were all reunited, and doing well.

"Oh, aren't they precious," Rosie said. "Now, tell me how you're feeling, Mary."

"Like I haven't slept in a month," Mary said, attempting to tidy up while keeping an eye on the twins and pacifying Elvis, who was now trying to climb up her leg. "I don't know how people do this, Mum. I feel like I'm drowning."

Rosie's maternal instincts kicked in. She was seriously out of practice, but she couldn't bear to see her daughter struggling like this. "Here, let me help," she said, moving to sit beside the children on the sofa.

"Thanks, Mum," Mary said, relief evident in her voice.

Rosie put her arms around both children, marvelling at how such small beings could simultaneously fill her with joy and trepidation. "There, there," she murmured, as they snuggled into her sides. To Rosie's surprise, both children seemed to calm in her presence and soon dropped off to sleep.

"How did you do that?" Mary asked, incredulous. "I've been trying to get them to sleep for hours."

Rosie shrugged, a small smile playing on her lips. "Just the magic touch, I suppose. Why don't you sit down? You look dead on your feet."

Mary collapsed into an armchair, watching the twins with a mixture of love and exhaustion.

"I don't know how much longer I can do this, Mum. Ted is away for another week, and I'm at my wit's end. I haven't showered in days, the house is a disaster, and don't even get me started on poor Elvis. I haven't walked him properly in ages."

As if understanding he was the topic of conversation, Elvis trotted over to Mary, head cocked to one side. He dropped a leash at her feet and looked up expectantly. Mary groaned. "Oh, Elvis, not now. I'm sorry, boy, but I just can't."

Rosie watched as Mary's eyes filled with tears. She remembered those early days of motherhood - the bone-deep exhaustion, the feeling of being overwhelmed, the guilt that came with not being able to do it all. But she'd only had Mary to contend with. Twins and a dog? It was no wonder her daughter was at breaking point. Before she could stop herself, Rosie heard herself say, "I could walk Elvis for you."

Mary's head snapped up. "What? Oh, Mum, I couldn't ask you to do that."

"You're not asking, I'm offering," Rosie said, surprising herself. She hadn't so much as petted a dog since the neighbour's old Labrador, Biscuit, had passed away years ago. But desperate times called for desperate measures. "It's no trouble. You focus on the twins, and I'll make sure Elvis gets some exercise."

"Are you sure?" Mary asked, hope creeping into her voice. "He can be a handful..."

Rosie waved away her concerns. "Nonsense. How hard can it be to walk a little dog like Elvis? It'll do me good to get some fresh air."

Twenty minutes later, Rosie found herself wondering if

she'd made a terrible mistake. Elvis pranced ahead of her, tugging on the leash with surprising strength for such a small dog. They'd barely made it to the end of Mary's street, and already Rosie was out of breath.

"Heel, Elvis," she commanded, trying to remember the dog training shows she used to watch. Elvis ignored her completely, instead choosing that moment to stop and thoroughly investigate a lamppost. Rosie sighed, glancing around furtively. The park at the end of the road was filled with fashionable young mothers pushing prams, joggers in skintight lycra, and professional dog walkers managing packs of well-behaved pooches. She felt painfully out of place in her sensible shoes and conservative outfit.

A young woman jogged past, flashing Rosie a pitying smile. "Cute dog," she called over her shoulder. "Is he your granddog?" Rosie felt her cheeks flush. Granddog? Did she look that old? She caught her reflection in the cafe window and gasped. When did she start looking like her own grandmother?

Elvis chose that moment to give the leash a particularly forceful tug, nearly yanking Rosie off her feet. She stumbled, arms windmilling as she fought to keep her balance. "Oh, for heaven's sake," she muttered, finally regaining her footing. She glared down at Elvis, who looked back at her with an expression of pure innocence. "Don't give me that look. I'm onto you, you little furball."

As she walked on, Rosie's discomfort grew. She felt like every eye was on her - the old lady who couldn't control one tiny dog. A group of mothers with children eyed her warily as Elvis strained towards them, yapping excitedly.

"Sorry, sorry," Rosie apologised, trying to steer Elvis away. "He's just... friendly."

One of the mothers, a willowy blonde in designer athleisure wear, raised an eyebrow. "You might want to try a harness," she said, her tone dripping with condescension. "It gives you more control."

Rosie bristled. More control? She'd raised a child, run a successful secretarial business, and navigated a divorce. She could handle one small dog, thank you very much. But as Elvis darted from bush to bush, wrapped the leash around her legs, and generally made a nuisance of himself, Rosie's confidence waned. She was sweating now, her carefully styled hair coming loose in the light breeze.

"Elvis, please," she pleaded, trying to untangle herself for the umpteenth time. "Can't we just have a nice, calm walk?"

Elvis responded by spotting a squirrel and taking off at full speed. Caught off guard, Rosie was dragged along, her sensible shoes slipping on the damp grass. "Stop! Heel! Sit!" She tried every command she could think of, but Elvis was on a mission.

The squirrel darted up a tree, and Elvis came to an abrupt halt at its base. The sudden stop sent Rosie stumbling forward, and before she knew it, she was face-down on the ground, her dignity in tatters along with her beige cardigan. For a moment, she lay there, the cool grass against her cheek, wondering how on earth she'd ended up in this situation. Then, she felt a warm, wet tongue on her face. She opened her eyes to find Elvis looking at her with what she could have sworn was concern.

Despite herself, Rosie chuckled. "Well, this is a fine mess you've gotten us into," she said, pushing herself up to a sitting position.

Elvis wagged his tail, then promptly flopped down next to her, resting his head on her lap. As Rosie sat there, grass stains on her knees and Elvis contentedly snuggled against her, she realised something. For the first time in years, she felt... alive. Her heart was racing, her cheeks were flushed, and despite the embarrassment, she felt a spark of something she hadn't experienced in a long time. Excitement? Adventure?

She looked around the park with new eyes. Yes, there were the perfect young mothers and the fit dog walkers. But there were also older couples strolling hand in hand, groups of friends laughing on benches, and solo wanderers lost in thought. She loved the way they were all in such lovely, bright clothing. When was the last time she'd worn something colourful? Her wardrobe consisted of every shade of beige. In an effort to look sophisticated, she'd ended up looking downright frumpy.

Right, in future she would embrace colour. With a renewed sense of determination, Rosie got to her feet, brushing grass from her clothes. "Alright, Elvis," she said, a glint in her eye. "Let's try this again, shall we? And this time, we play by my rules."

As they set off down the path, Rosie held her head high. Let them stare. Let them wonder about the sixty-something woman with grass in her hair and a mischievous dog by her side. She had a feeling this was just the beginning of something new and exciting.

By the time they returned to Mary's house, Rosie was dishevelled, tired, and covered in dog hair - but she was also grinning from ear to ear. She walked into the house and collapsed on the sofa. Elvis curled up by her feet and fell asleep. Mary felt a wave of affection for the little dog.

"I'll get you a cup of tea," said Mary. "The twins are napping, so I've got a moment to think straight.

While Mary headed into the kitchen, Rosie leaned over and picked up a photo album lying on the coffee table. Her fingers traced the edge of the cover, hesitating before she opened it. There, on the first page, was a picture that never failed to make her heart skip: Her estranged husband, Derek, cradling their newborn daughter Mary, his face a mixture of awe and terror.

She remembered how they'd counted each tiny finger and toe, marvelling at the perfection of this little being they'd created.

"Ten and ten," Derek had whispered, his voice choked with emotion. "She's got all her bits, Ro. We did good."

"Here, one cup of tea," said Mary. "Sorry – I should have put that photo album away. It's full of pictures of you and dad."

"Oh, don't be daft, your father and I split up a long time ago, it's all in the past. No hard feelings. He's with Pauline now."

"No he's not. He split up with Pauline ages ago. I assumed you knew."

Pauline was the woman who Derek had left her for. She was a former friend and their romance had left Rosie feeling completely betrayed.

"Sorry, I didn't mean to upset you," said Mary. "I honestly thought you knew, mum."

"No, it's fine. I'm not upset at all. Just surprised. Why did they split up?"

"If you want the truth, I think he's still in love with you."

"Don't be silly."

"No, I mean it. He's always asking after you."

"That's because I'm your mother."

"No, it's more than that."

Rosie went quiet so Mary swung the conversation into something less emotional.

"How was the walk?" she asked.

"It was great. Lovely to get some fresh air and be out and about. I really enjoyed it."

"Oh good," said Mary.

"Same time tomorrow?" Rosie asked, surprising both Mary and herself.

Mary's eyes widened. "Really? You'd do that?"

Rosie nodded, a newfound resolve settling over her. "Absolutely. Elvis and I have some unfinished business in that park."

As she drove home, Rosie couldn't shake the feeling that something had shifted. She glanced at herself in the rearview mirror, taking in her wind-tousled hair and the spark in her eyes. She felt more alive than she had in ages. She'd loved walking the dog. She found herself looking forward to tomorrow.

PARK BENCH CONFESSIONS

*H*ands on hips, Rosie surveyed the sea of beige, navy, and cream before her. Was this really all she owned? When had her closet become as exciting as a rice cake?

"Right," she muttered, pushing hangers aside with newfound determination. "There has to be something here that doesn't scream 'sensible grandmother.'"

After what felt like an archaeological dig through layers of conservative cardigans and practical slacks, Rosie's hand brushed against something silky. She pulled it out, eyebrows rising at the sight of a leopard print blouse she'd forgotten she owned. "Well, hello there," she said, a slow smile spreading across her face. "Where have you been hiding?"

Fifteen minutes later, Rosie appraised herself in the full-length mirror. The leopard print blouse, paired with black jeans she'd had to wiggle into (when did these get so tight?), and a pair of red ballet flats gave her an air of... what was the word? Sass? She nodded at her reflection. Yes, that would do.

As she headed out the door, Rosie caught sight of herself in the hallway mirror and faltered. Was this too much?

Should she change back into something more... age-appropriate? The familiar voice in her head whispered that she was being ridiculous to think she could get away with a blouse like that.

But Rosie squared her shoulders, fixing her reflection with a steely gaze. "Oh, hush," she told the voices. "I'm sixty, not dead."

With that, she marched out the door, trying to channel the confidence of her blouse. Rosie walked to Mary's house. It was a shorter stroll than she had thought it would be...she was so used to driving that she'd forgotten how lovely it felt to walk. Certainly, the newfound spring in her step made the distance fly by. As she approached the familiar door, it swung open before she could knock, revealing a marginally less frazzled-looking Mary.

"Mum!" Mary's eyes widened as she took in Rosie's outfit. "You look... different."

Rosie felt her cheeks warm. "Good different or bad different?"

A slow smile spread across Mary's face. "Good different. Definitely good. You look great, Mum."

Before Rosie could respond, a shaggy blonde bullet shot out from behind Mary's legs. Elvis, apparently recognising his new walking companion, launched himself at Rosie with all the enthusiasm of a long-lost friend.

"Down, boy!" Rosie laughed, trying to fend off Elvis's enthusiastic greeting. "Save some of that energy for the park, why don't you?"

Mary handed over the leash, shaking her head in amazement. "I still can't believe you're doing this, Mum. Are you sure you're up for it?"

Rosie took the leash, giving Mary a reassuring pat on the arm. "Absolutely. Elvis and I have an understanding now, don't we, boy?"

She looked down at the dog, who cocked his head and gave a small 'woof' in response.

"Well, good luck," Mary said, stifling a yawn. "I'm going to try and catch up on a million tonnes of washing."

As Rosie set off towards the park, she felt a curious mix of excitement and trepidation. Yesterday's walk had been a comedy of errors, but today... today she was prepared. Or so she thought. Elvis trotted alongside her, mercifully calm compared to yesterday's escapades.

As they entered the park, Rosie held her head high, pointedly ignoring the curious glances her leopard print blouse was attracting. They made it halfway around the pond before Elvis decided it was time to liven things up. A flock of ducks caught his attention, and before Rosie could tighten her grip on the leash, he was off like a shot.

"Elvis, no!" Rosie yelped, stumbling after him. The ducks scattered in a flurry of indignant quacks, while Elvis barked joyfully, clearly thinking this was the best game ever.

Rosie's red ballet flats, it turned out, were not designed for impromptu duck chases. She felt her foot slide on the damp grass, and for the second time in as many days, she found herself heading for an unplanned meeting with the ground. Just as she braced for impact, a strong hand gripped her arm, steadying her.

"Whoa there! I've got you."

Rosie looked up into the amused face of a woman about her age, with dark blonde hair in a bob. She had laughter lines around her eyes and a big smile on her face.

"That's some dog you've got there," the woman said, nodding towards Elvis, now prancing proudly among the retreating ducks.

"He's not mine, actually," Rosie said, straightening up and trying to salvage what was left of her dignity. "I'm dog-walking for my daughter. Or rather, dog-falling."

The woman laughed, a rich, throaty sound that immediately put Rosie at ease. "Well, you're in good company. Half the people here can't manage their dogs. I'm Emma, by the way."

"Rosie," she replied, shaking Emma's offered hand. "And the four-legged menace over there is Elvis."

"Elvis, eh?" Emma grinned. "Let's see if we can't coax him back. I've got just the thing."

She rummaged in her pocket and pulled out a dog treat. With a sharp whistle, she called, "Here, Elvis! Come and get it, boy!" To Rosie's amazement, Elvis's ears perked up, and he came bounding over, all thoughts of ducks forgotten. He sat obediently at Emma's feet, looking up with adoring eyes as she handed him the treat.

"How did you do that?" Rosie asked, impressed. Emma shrugged, giving Elvis a scratch behind the ears.

"The secret to a man's heart is through his stomach. Turns out it works for dogs too."

She glanced at Rosie's leopard print blouse and red shoes, a twinkle in her eye. "Love the outfit, by the way."

Rosie felt herself relax for the first time since leaving the house. "Thanks. I wasn't sure if it was too much, to be honest."

"Nonsense," Emma scoffed. "If you've got it, flaunt it. That's what I always say. Come on, why don't you join me and my friend Lisa? We were just about to have our morning coffee on that bench over there."

Rosie hesitated for a moment, then nodded. Why not? It wasn't as if she had a packed social calendar these days. As they approached the bench, Rosie saw another woman a little younger than them, elegantly dressed in a crisp white shirt and tailored trousers. She was tapping away on a sleek laptop, a furrow of concentration between her brows.

"Oi, Lisa!" Emma called out. "Pack that away, will you? We've got company."

Lisa looked up, pushing a pair of reading glasses onto her head. Her eyes widened slightly as she took in Rosie's outfit, but she smiled warmly.

"Well, hello there. I do hope Emma hasn't been terrorising you. She has that effect on unsuspecting park-goers."

"Oi!" Emma protested good-naturedly, plopping down on the bench. "I'll have you know I just saved Rosie here from a nasty fall. Elvis was making a break for it."

"Elvis?" Lisa raised an eyebrow, looking around. "I don't see any... oh!"

She laughed as the Cavapoo in question stuck his head out from behind Rosie's legs. "Hello, handsome."

"Rosie, sit down with your pretty dog. Tell me all about yourself."

"Well, there's not much to say really..."

"Whoah... stop right there. There will be loads to say. Stop putting yourself down before you've even started. That's not allowed. is it, Emma."

"No, it is not. Lisa has a thing about women putting themselves down. She likes women to be confident and self-assured."

"Oh blimey. It's been a long time since I was anywhere near confident or self-assured."

"OK then. I'm going to fire questions at you: are you married."

"No. I'm separated from my husband Derek."

"Any children?"

"One: a daughter called Mary. I have two grandchildren as well."

"What are their names?"

Emma put her hand out. "Stop interrogating the poor woman."

She turned to Rosie. "I'm sorry about my friend she interviews people and writes about them for a living. Every time she meets someone, she starts interviewing them like they're on Newsnight or something."

"I don't mind," said Rosie. In fact, she was quite enjoying it. No one ever asks you about yourself when you're over 60. They assume you're retired and spend your time knitting. It was refreshing to find two women who wanted to know about her.

"Good. Rosie doesn't mind, so I can carry on talking to her and you can butt out, Emma."

"OK, fair enough."

"So, Rosie. Where do you live?"

"Just on the High Street in the middle of Esher."

"Oh, very near us," said Emma. "I'm surprised we haven't met before."

"Do you work?" asked Lisa.

"I'm retired now. I used to work as a receptionist – in a doctor's surgery and in schools. I also had my own secretarial business at one stage, with a handful of employees. I enjoyed that."

"So, you had your own business, you have a daughter, grandchildren and fabulous taste in clothes. You've done OK for yourself," said Lisa. "Now tell us - what's the craziest thing you've ever done?"

Rosie felt like she was at the oddest job interview ever. "I went to Paris for my 60th with my daughter and we went to a cabaret club and got drunk. I went onto the stage and performed a can-can with the professional dancers."

The two women stood up and burst into rapturous applause. "You must never say 'there's not much to say' when people ask you to talk about yourself," said Emma.

"Always lead with the can-can," said Lisa. "That's my advice."

"Is that your general life advice, Lisa?" asked Emma.

"Pretty much."

"Now it's your turn...tell me everything," said Rosie.

"I'm 67," said Emma. "I used to run a nursery but sold the place and retired six months ago."

"Emma's the party queen," said Lisa. "I've never known anyone like her...she wants to play ALL THE TIME."

"That's true. Lisa's right," said Emma, fishing a cigarette out of her pocket and lighting it.

"And she shouldn't be smoking," said Lisa.

"I smoke, and I know I shouldn't. My ex-husband, Robert, used to hate me smoking, so I became a secret smoker. I'd have a packet of mints before going home just to disguise the smell. But then he started noticing the smell of mints and knew I'd been smoking, so I switched to blackcurrant cough sweets. They did the trick. He was none-the-wiser after that."

Emma was incredibly attractive – tall and, while not slim, had a good figure and a pretty face – sparkling green eyes shone out from a face unadorned with make-up. Perfect skin, perfect teeth and the biggest smile Rosie had ever seen. She seemed to have no interest in dressing up. Her clothes were thrown together with cheerful disregard for fashion, while her wit was sharp and her personality thoroughly engaging.

"Your turn, Lisa," said Emma.

"OK, well – I'm 60, and..."

"60?" gasped Rosie. "There is no way on this earth that you are 60."

"I am," said Lisa.

"Well then – I need to know all your beauty secrets. You look like you're in your 40s for God's sake."

Lisa was very petite and sort of 'neat', with perfectly manicured nails, hair in a sleek, shiny bob and tanned skin. She looked like a TV presenter.

"I've had a few bits of work done, I'll confess. I'm from

Majorca originally and have a lovely doctor there who helps with wrinkle eradication," she said.

In one sentence Lisa had explained the colour and youthfulness of her skin. Rosie nodded wisely, visioning a quick trip to Majorca, and returning with flawless, tanned skin.

"Are you still working?" asked Rosie. "You seem much too young to have retired."

"I'm a writer and biographer. I tend to do mainly politicians' memoirs and a bit of speech writing these days. I was a political commentator for The Times when I was younger."

"Wow," said Rosie. She'd never met anyone with such a glamorous job.

"And she sometimes gets to socialise with the politicians, so that's nice, isn't it?" said Emma, earning herself a sharp look from Lisa.

"OK, I'll be honest, I have been known to have the odd fling," Lisa confessed. "But I live alone, I've been divorced from William for two decades. Why shouldn't I?"

"Why, indeed?" said Rosie. "But don't most of them look like they've been fashioned out of uncooked dough."

Lisa laughed. "Very true."

"How did you two meet?" asked Rosie. "And what are you doing hanging around in the park?"

"We hang around in the park because I come here to write sometimes, and I convinced Emma to come down and hang out with me because she never gets any fresh air. We met through Emma's nursery. I helped a neighbour out by picking her children up from nursery from time to time, and we became friends."

"Do you have any children yourself?" Rosie asked.

"No, sadly not. I'd have loved that, but it never happened."

Lisa moved the conversation on quickly, and Rosie regretted asking.

"Do you walk the dog here often? I don't think I've seen you here before."

Rosie launched into the tale of how she'd ended up as Elvis's reluctant dog walker, finding herself embellishing the story of yesterday's misadventures as Emma and Lisa dissolved into peals of laughter.

"Oh my," Lisa wiped a tear from her eye. "I haven't laughed like that in ages. Bless you, Rosie. We needed that."

As the laughter subsided, Rosie found herself studying her new acquaintances. Despite their obvious differences, there was an easy camaraderie between them that made her feel a pang of... was it loneliness?

"So, do you two come here often?" Rosie asked, immediately cringing at how much it sounded like a pickup line.

Emma snorted. "Every damn day," she said. "Lisa won't see me indoors because of her insane belief in fresh air."

"Will you be coming every day, now?"

"Yes I will, now I'm the head dog walker," said Rosie.

"Are you married? I can't remember what you said."

"No. I'm separated from Derek. He had an affair, but I heard this morning that the affair has been over for some time. I don't know. It's... complicated."

"Isn't it always?" Lisa sighed. "I'm in the same boat. William - that's my ex - he decided that after thirty years of marriage, he'd rather trade me in for a younger model. I was getting too 'set in my ways'."

"Men," Emma scoffed. "Can't live with 'em, can't bury 'em in the back garden without awkward questions from the neighbours."

Rosie found herself laughing again, a weight she hadn't realised she'd been carrying starting to lift. "It's not easy, is it? Starting over at our age."

"Tell me about it," Emma groaned. "Do you know, I considered online dating the other day? Can you imagine?

Me, trying to sum up sixty years of life in a little box, competing with women half my age who don't need industrial-strength support knickers."

Lisa nearly choked on her coffee. "Emma! You didn't!"

"I didn't," Emma admitted. "Came to my senses before I clicked 'submit'. But still, a woman has needs, you know?"

"Oh, I know," Rosie surprised herself by saying. "The other day, I caught myself eyeing up the young man delivering my groceries. I mean, really eyeing him up. I was mortified."

"Why?" Emma asked, genuinely puzzled. "Nothing wrong with window shopping, love. It's not like you tried to lure him, Mrs Robinson style."

"Although," Lisa mused, a wicked glint in her eye, "if I go much longer without sex, that's exactly what I'll be doing."

The three women looked at each other for a beat before bursting into laughter again.

"You know what the worst part is?" Lisa said, her tone turning contemplative. "It's not even the loneliness. It's feeling... invisible. Like the world has moved on and forgotten about you."

Emma nodded solemnly. "I know what you mean. The other day, I was in the supermarket, and this young thing asked if I needed help reaching something on the top shelf. I'm 5'10" for heaven's sake! I wanted to tell her I could not only reach the top shelf but probably bench press her skinny arse if I wanted to. I know it was kind of her and she meant well, but we all know that she only offered because I'm old. That really got to me."

"But I bet you didn't say anything, did you?" Lisa asked.

"No," Emma sighed. "I just smiled and said no thank you. And then I went home and ate an entire tub of ice cream."

Rosie felt a lump form in her throat. "I thought it was just me," she said quietly. "Feeling... obsolete."

There was a moment of silence, broken only by Elvis's contented snoring at their feet. Then Emma straightened up, a determined look on her face.

"Right, that's enough of that. We're not obsolete, we're... vintage. Like a fine wine. Or a classic car."

"Or a well-aged cheese?" Lisa suggested with a smirk.

"Exactly!" Emma exclaimed. "We're not over the hill, we're just getting started. Who says we can't have adventures? Who says we can't turn heads?" Rosie found herself nodding, caught up in Emma's enthusiasm. "You're right. We're not dead yet."

"That's the spirit!" Emma beamed. "Now, what do you say we make this a regular thing? Same time tomorrow? We can swap stories, complain about our aches and pains, ogle the young fathers pushing prams..."

"Emma!" Lisa admonished, but she was smiling.

Rosie hesitated for a moment, then nodded decisively. "I'd like that. Very much."

As they exchanged phone numbers and made plans to meet for coffee the next day, Rosie felt a spark of excitement. Maybe this dog-walking gig wasn't such a bad idea after all.

When it was time to leave, Rosie stood up, giving Elvis's leash a gentle tug. To her surprise, he got up without protest, looking up at her with what she could have sworn was a smug expression.

"I think Elvis here might be a good luck charm," Emma observed. "Bringing people together and all that."

As she said her goodbyes and started to walk away, Lisa called out, "Oh, and Rosie? Wear that blouse again tomorrow. It suits you." Rosie felt a warm glow of pleasure as she waved goodbye. "I might show you my can-can," she shouted.

She was looking forward to tomorrow. Who knew what adventures it might bring? After all, she was sixty, sassy, and just getting started.

. . .

"How are you doing, sweetheart?" asked Derek.

"Oh, hi dad, I'm fine," said Mary.

"It sounds suspiciously quiet there."

"Yes – the twins have fallen asleep. Mum was over earlier and wove some sort of magic spell on them. They fell asleep straight away."

"Rosie's there?"

"She was. She's just taken Elvis for a walk."

"What? Taken Elvis?"

"Yes. She took him yesterday as well."

"Really? I didn't know she liked dogs. I always wanted to get one, but she was never interested."

"No, she surprised me, too."

"Do you know where she's gone? I could head out and catch up with her."

"No, I'm not sure. And I think she'll be back soon."

"Back to your house?"

"Yes."

"Shall I come round?"

"I don't think that's a good idea, dad."

"OK. Well, I'll let you get on with things then. I might pop around for coffee later if that's OK? I might be able to help out. Perhaps take Elvis out again?"

"Sure."

Her father hung up, and Mary smiled to herself. This poor little dog was all set to have more walks than ever by the sound of it...caught in the middle as her father pursued her mother. Were all families as complicated as hers?

PARK BENCH CHRONICLES

The late summer sun dappled the path through the park as Rosie made her way to what had become, over the past few weeks, her favourite bench. A few months ago she'd never have imagined having a favourite bench, or sit on a bench of any kind. But over the past few weeks she had arranged to meet the women every day.

They'd chatted endlessly and shared all sorts of views… what they loved, what they hated and where they saw their lives going.

She'd bumped into Derek in the park a few times, which had annoyed her. She loved the idea of this park being her domain…somewhere that she and her new friends could hang out.

Derek had been lovely to her, and charm personified to Lisa and Emma, of course. They'd thought he was great until she reminded them that Derek had an affair with one of her friends.

Rosie recognised that Derek was still a fine-looking man. He was 6 feet tall and held himself extremely well, standing bolt upright so he looked taller. His frame, while still holding the memory of athletic prowess, bore the softness of a man who had long since traded the gym for the boardroom, but there was something attractive and slightly comforting about that.

His face was etched with the lines of countless corporate battles, each wrinkle a testament to deals won and lost. In speech, he was bright but reserved, his words carefully measured.

He had this air of authority, or faded authority was more accurate, like a once-grand building now slightly worn at the edges.

Elvis had greeted Derek with considerable enthusiasm, jumping up, eager to be stroked. Today he trotted along by her side, much better behaved since she'd started walking him. The last month had been a learning experience for both of them.

That first outing had been chaotic, but she had come to the park most days since then and they'd formed a lovely partnership. The only time he became unmanageable now was when he saw a squirrel. Then he charged through the park like a maniac. Rosie smiled to herself, remembering that first morning and how out of her depth she felt. Now, her walks with him were filled with laughter, unexpected adventures, and a growing sense of liberation.

As she rounded the corner, she saw Emma already there, resplendent in a flowing kaftan that seemed to catch every ray of sunlight. Emma waved enthusiastically, nearly knocking Lisa's hat off in the process.

"Rosie, darling! We were just placing bets on whether you'd wear that darling blouse from yesterday again. You do have some of the loveliest clothes," Emma called out.

Lisa chuckled, adjusting her hat. "I told her you were too

fashion-conscious for that. Though I must say, that yellow sundress is a knockout. Suits you perfectly."

Rosie felt a warm glow of pleasure at the compliment. She was still getting used to dressing for herself rather than for Derek's approval or to blend in at the charity committee meetings.

"Well, I had excellent advisors," Rosie replied with a wink as she settled onto the bench. "Though I did get a few raised eyebrows at the post office this morning."

"Raised eyebrows are just a sign you're doing something right," a woman interjected, appearing as if by magic with a tray of iced coffees. "I'm Becky. I'm from the café just along the river. Nice to meet you."

"Oh, nice to meet you, too," said Rosie. "Which café is that?"

"It's called Becky's. Just by the bridge."

"Oh yes, of course. Thanks very much."

As they sipped their coffees, Becky pulled out a bulging folder. "I was just finalising the itinerary for your day trip to Brighton next week."

Emma raised an eyebrow. "Itinerary? Darling, the only items on my Brighton itinerary are 'arrive' and 'have fun'."

"Oh, but I've researched all the best spots!" Becky protested. "I told you I used to live there, and you asked me to design the perfect Brighton day for you."

"I'm only joking. We're very grateful," said Emma.

"Right. Well, there's a lovely tearoom that's been operating since 1907 and a quaint little museum about the history of—"

"Nooooo," said Emma. "I don't want to go to tea rooms."

How about we split the difference?" Rosie suggested diplomatically. "We can visit the tearoom for lunch, but maybe leave some room for spontaneity too?"

Becky looked uncertain, but nodded. "I suppose that

could work. As long as you're back in time for the 5:15 train. I've already bought the tickets."

The others exchanged amused glances. Becky's obsession with planning was a running joke for Emma and Lisa, but they all appreciated her attention to detail. She wanted to become a travel coordinator – planning trips to far-flung locations for high-net-worth individuals. Organising a trip to Brighton for three sixty-year-olds was a tame start, but everyone had to start somewhere.

Becky left and Rosie chatted to Emma, while Lisa appeared to be sketching something. Suddenly she held up her pad.

"Ladies, I give you 'The Sassy Sixties Squad in all their glory!"

Emma and Rosie looked thrilled. She'd captured the two of them perfectly – Emma's flamboyant gestures, and Rosie's newfound confidence.

"Oh, Lisa," Rosie breathed, "it's wonderful. You've made us look so... vibrant."

"I just drew what I saw," Lisa replied with a shrug, but her eyes twinkled with pleasure.

As the sun began to dip lower in the sky, casting long shadows across the park, Emma clapped her hands.

"Right, ladies. Who's up for a little adventure?"

"Yes!" Lisa exclaimed. "Bring me wild adventures."

"I said a 'little adventure' not a 'wild adventure'. I was just going to suggest a bite to eat and a glass of wine?"

"Yes, good thinking. There's a new little bistro that's opened up on the high street. I say we give it a try," said Lisa.

There was a moment of hesitation – each woman mentally running through her usual evening routine – before Rosie spoke up. "Oh, why not? Life's too short to always play it safe." As they gathered their things, Rosie felt a surge of excitement. A month ago, the idea of an impromptu dinner out would have filled her with anxiety. Now, she found herself looking forward to the unexpected.

Her pre-married life had been a long sequence of drinks, dinners and fun with friends. How soon all that stopped when you had children. Her life as a wife and mother had been all about a calendar in the kitchen filled with pre-booked activities. The fun of deciding to do something, and just doing it was a thrill she'd almost forgotten.

She texted Mary to tell her she was taking Elvis out to dinner, and joined the others for the short walk. The bistro was called 'Jools.' It turned out to be a wonderful little place, all cosy with mismatched furniture and twinkling fairy lights strung across the ceiling.

"Ladies," said a handsome young waiter. "What can I do for you?"

"For God's sake, don't ask that of a group of menopausal women," said Emma. "You don't know what answer you'll get."

The waiter gave a smile which appeared welcoming on the surface but carried with it a whiff of nervousness.

For reasons that weren't entirely clear to the other women, Emma then began regaling him with the outrageous tale about Rosie's days as a cabaret dancer in Paris.

"Not true, not true," Rosie yelled. "I just got up onto the stage once to do the cancan because I was very drunk, it was my 60th birthday and I'd just found out that my husband was having an affair. I wasn't a full-time can-can dancer."

"Well, for what it's worth, I think your husband must be mad," said the waiter.

The women all cheered, Elvis looked at Rosie quizzically from his seat at the end of the banquette, Rosie looked at Emma and smiled, and everyone in the bistro looked over at them.

"We're having more fun than anyone else in the world

right now," said Emma. "We're relaxed, happy, surrounded by friends and we don't need anyone or anything, Life is magnificent."

"To new friends and new adventures," Rosie toasted.

"And to the Sassy Sixties squad!" Emma added with a wink.

CAFFEINE AND CAMARADERIE

Rosie picked up the colourful jug and poured herself a glass of water. Since she'd met Emma and Lisa, she felt so much more confident about herself.

She'd started buying brighter, more vibrant furniture for the house, and dressing in ways which attracted attention. She loved playing with colours, styles and fabrics. She smiled, fingering the sleeve of her crimson blouse.

Her phone buzzed, and she glanced at the screen to see a message from Emma: "Don't you dare show up in anything sensible. We're painting the town red... well, pale pink at least. It is only 11am after all."

Rosie chuckled, pleased she had chosen to wear the incredibly bright blouse.

"Challenge accepted, Emma," she murmured to herself.

Twenty minutes later, Rosie found herself outside The Bean Counter, a trendy coffee shop in the high street. The exterior was all sleek lines and minimalist decor, a far cry from Jools, the cosy bistro.

She peered through the window, spotting Emma at a table near the back. Lisa sat beside her, looking as polished as ever in a tailored blazer. Two other women who Rosie didn't recognise completed the group. Taking a deep breath, she pushed open the door, the scent of freshly ground coffee beans enveloping her. As she approached the table, Emma looked up and let out a wolf whistle. "Well, well, well," Emma grinned, eyeing Rosie's outfit appreciatively. "Look who's embracing her inner fire engine."

Rosie felt her cheeks warm to match her blouse. "Is it too much?" she asked, suddenly self-conscious.

"Nonsense," Lisa interjected, standing to greet Rosie with a warm hug. "You look fabulous. That deep pink is definitely your colour."

"Hear, hear," one of the unfamiliar women chimed in. She was a petite blonde with a head of curly hair, tied at the nape of her neck and piles of jewellery on her wrists, around her neck and dangling from her ears. She had an artistic air about her.

"I'm Julie. Emma's told us all about you."

"All good things, I hope," Rosie said, taking the empty seat between Julie and the other newcomer.

"Oh, the best," the other woman said with a wink. She was curvy and warm-looking, with a slightly harried air that reminded Rosie of Mary. "I'm Catherine."

Catherine seemed a bit different from the other women. Shyer and nowhere near as elegantly dressed. She wore denim dungarees and kept fiddling with her fingernails.

"We are the 'Sensational Sixties Squad' now," Emma said.

Rosie raised an eyebrow at Emma, who shrugged unapologetically. "What? We needed a catchy name. Anyway, it was Lisa who came up with it, with her painting of us. Now, who's for coffee?"

As they perused the menu, Rosie felt her eyes widening at the array of options. What on earth was a 'Unicorn Frappuccino'? And since when did coffee need to be 'deconstructed'?

"Right," Emma said, clapping her hands together. "Let's make this interesting. We each order for the person to our right, and it has to be the most ridiculous thing on the menu."

"Oh, I don't know," Catherine fretted, biting her lip. "I'm not very good with complicated orders. What if I get it wrong?"

"That's half the fun," Lisa assured her with a pat on the arm. "Besides, how hard can it be? It's just coffee."

As it turned out, it could be very hard indeed. Julie went first, ordering for Catherine.

"She'll have a... um... Venti half-caf soy vanilla latte with an extra shot, upside down, with caramel drizzle and whipped cream."

The barista, a young man with more piercings than Rosie had ever seen on one person, didn't bat an eye as he scribbled the order down.

Catherine, looking slightly panicked, ordered for Lisa. "A grande... no, venti... oh, dear. A big iced skinny hazelnut macchiato, sugar-free syrup, extra shot, light ice, no whip."

Lisa nodded approvingly. "Not bad, Catherine. You're a natural."

When it was Lisa's turn to order for Emma, she got a mischievous glint in her eye.

"She'll have a trenta cold brew, five shots, with vanilla sweet cream foam, two pumps of mocha, one pump of white mocha, extra caramel drizzle, and cinnamon dolce topping."

Emma's eyes widened. "Good lord, woman. Are you trying to give me a heart attack?"

"Just keeping you on your toes, dear," Lisa replied sweetly.

Emma turned to order for Rosie. "Right, let's see... She'll have a venti soy no foam light-roast half-caf with a splash of sugar-free vanilla and a twist of lemon. Oh, and make it extra hot."

Rosie blinked, trying to process the string of words that had just assaulted her ears.

"I'm sorry, did you just order me coffee or summon a demon?"

The table erupted in laughter, drawing curious glances from nearby patrons. When it was Rosie's turn to order for Julie, she felt a bead of sweat form on her brow. "Um... she'll have a... oh, bollocks. Can I just point at something on the menu?"

The barista, to his credit, maintained his professional demeanour, though Rosie could have sworn she saw the corner of his mouth twitch.

"How about a Unicorn Frappuccino?" he suggested kindly. "It's... colourful."

"Perfect," Rosie said, relieved. "One of those, please. And maybe a shot of whiskey for me?"

As the barista moved away to prepare their drinks, Emma leaned in conspiratorially. "So, ladies, now that we're all acquainted, let's get down to the good stuff. Who's got the best ex-husband horror story?"

"Oh, don't get me started," Catherine groaned. "Richard - that's my ex - he's an army officer. Emphasis on the 'officer' part. The man can't so much as butter his toast without barking orders."

"At least he butters his own toast," Julie chimed in. "My Tom - well, we're separated, not divorced yet - he once called me from the next room to ask where we keep the forks. We've lived in the same house for twenty years!"

Lisa shook her head sympathetically. "Men. Can't live with them, can't legally feed them to the pigs."

"Not that you've checked, of course," Emma said with a wink.

"Of course not," Lisa replied primly, then ruined the effect by adding, "Hypothetically speaking, it's the teeth you've got to worry about. They don't... I mean, I've heard they don't digest well."

"What about you, Rosie?" Julie asked, wiping tears of mirth from her eyes. "Any ex-husband tales to share?"

Rosie hesitated, fiddling with a napkin. "Well, Derek and I... it's complicated. We're separated, but he's been making noises about wanting to reconcile. My "daughter said that he still loves me.

"And do you want to?" Catherine asked gently.

Before Rosie could answer, their drinks arrived - a kaleidoscope of colours, textures, and aromas that looked more like science experiments than beverages.

"Good grief," Emma exclaimed, eyeing her monstrosity of a drink. "I think mine just winked at me."

Julie poked at her drink with a straw, watching in fascination as the colours swirled. "I'm not sure whether to drink this or hang it in my gallery."

As they cautiously sampled their concoctions, pulling faces and swapping sips, Rosie felt a warmth that had nothing to do with her 'extra hot' coffee.

"You never answered the question, you know," Lisa said softly, nudging Rosie's arm. "About Derek."

Rosie sighed, staring into the depths of her bizarre coffee creation. "Honestly? I don't know. We were together for so long, it's hard to imagine life without him. But at the same time..." she trailed off, struggling to find the words.

"At the same time, you can't help but wonder what else is out there?" Emma finished for her.

Rosie nodded, relieved that someone understood.

"Exactly. It's like... I've been 'Derek's wife' for so long, I'm not sure I remember how to just be 'Rosie' anymore."

"Oh, honey," Catherine reached across the table to squeeze Rosie's hand. "We've all been there. When Richard left, I didn't know how to do anything for myself. I mean, the man had been choosing my clothes for years. Can you believe that?"

Julie nodded emphatically. "I get it. When Tom moved out, I stared at the washing machine for an hour because I couldn't remember how to use it. He'd always done the laundry."

"See, that's the thing," Lisa interjected. "We get so used to being one half of a couple that we forget how to be whole on our own. But let me tell you something, ladies - we are not half of anything. We are whole, complete, fabulous women."

"Hear, hear!" Emma raised her ridiculous coffee in a toast. "To being whole, complete, and fabulous!"

As they clinked their mugs together, Rosie felt a surge of affection for these women she barely knew. They were all so different - Emma with her irreverent humour, Lisa with her polished exterior and hidden mischief, Julie with her artistic soul, and Catherine with her endearing mix of anxiety and warmth. Yet somehow, they fit together perfectly.

"You know," Rosie said, surprising herself, "I think I'm going to tell Derek no. About getting back together, I mean."

The table fell silent, all eyes on Rosie.

"Are you sure?" Catherine asked. "That's a big decision."

Rosie nodded, feeling more certain with each passing second. "I am. It's time for me to figure out who I am without him. And I have a feeling it's going to be someone pretty amazing."

"That's my girl!" Emma crowed, reaching over to high-five Rosie. "Look out world, Rosie 2.0 is coming!"

As the conversation flowed, moving from ex-husbands to empty nests ("I swear, I can hear my echo in the house now," Julie lamented), to dreams they'd put on hold ("I always wanted to learn the tango," Catherine admitted shyly), Rosie felt a sense of possibility unfurling within her.

"Ladies," Lisa said suddenly, setting down her coffee with a decisive thunk. "I have a proposition for you."

"Ooh, sounds scandalous," Emma waggled her eyebrows. "Do tell."

Lisa rolled her eyes good-naturedly. "Nothing so exciting, I'm afraid. But I was thinking... what if we made this a regular thing? Not just coffee, but... adventures?"

"Adventures?" Catherine echoed, looking both intrigued and terrified.

"Yes, adventures," Lisa nodded enthusiastically. "We're all at a crossroads, aren't we? Kids grown up, marriages ended or ending, careers winding down. But that doesn't mean our lives are over. Far from it. I say it's time we start living again, really living."

"I'm in," Emma said immediately. "God knows I could use some excitement that doesn't involve arguing with the meter reader."

Julie nodded slowly, a smile spreading across her face. "You know what? Why not? My gallery can run itself for a few hours a week."

All eyes turned to Catherine, who was chewing her lip nervously. "I don't know... I'm not very adventurous. What if I make a fool of myself?"

"Then you'll be in good company," Rosie found herself saying. "Because I have a feeling we're all going to make fools of ourselves at some point. But won't it be fun?"

Catherine looked at each of them in turn, then squared her shoulders. "Alright, I'm in. But if we end up skydiving or something, I'm blaming all of you."

As they laughed and began throwing out ideas for their future 'adventures' ("Pottery class!" "Wine tasting!" "Naked life drawing - as the artists, not the models, Emma!"), Rosie felt a bubble of excitement building in her chest. Why should the young have all the fun?

As they gathered their things to leave, Rosie caught sight of their reflection in the coffee shop window. Five women, all in their sixties, all laughing and chattering like schoolgirls. But there was a strength there too, a resilience born of lives fully lived and challenges overcome.

"The Sensational Sixties Squad," she murmured to herself, testing the words out. "You know what? I think I like it." And with that, Rosie stepped out into the sunshine, ready to embrace whatever adventures lay ahead. After all, sixty was just a number. The real journey was only just beginning.

YOGA CATASTROPHE

Rosie stood in front of her full-length mirror, tugging at the unfamiliar spandex clinging to her body. The yoga pants and tank top ensemble she'd panic-bought the day before left little to the imagination.

"Good lord," she muttered, turning sideways and sucking in her stomach. "I look like a sausage trying to escape its casing."

Her phone buzzed with a message from Emma: "Don't you dare back out, Red. If I'm squeezing into lycra, so are you."

Rosie chuckled, shaking her head.

"Why are you calling me red?"

"My new name for you…you wear bright clothes and you are a bright soul."

Rosie responded with a 'x'. There was no backing out now. The Sensational Sixties Squad's first official adventure was about to begin.

She grabbed her hastily purchased yoga mat and headed out the door, her mind buzzing with thoughts.

Yoga?

At her age?

How could that possibly be a good idea?

The Zen Garden Yoga Studio looked like it had been plucked straight from a lifestyle magazine. All blonde wood and hanging plants, with a faint scent of lavender in the air. Rosie felt distinctly out of place as she navigated around bendy twenty-somethings in coordinated outfits.

She spotted her friends huddled near the back of the room, looking about as comfortable as cats at a dog show. Emma's huge smile stood out among the sea of serious faces and sleek ponytails, while Lisa appeared to be attempting to hide behind a potted fern.

"There you are!" Julie waved Rosie over, her artistic nature somehow at odds with the pristine white yoga outfit she'd chosen. Already, a smudge of what looked suspiciously like paint marred the hem of her top.

"I can't believe I let you talk me into this," Catherine hissed, trying unsuccessfully to cover her midriff with her arms. "I haven't shown this much skin since 1975."

"Oh, hush," Emma said, though Rosie noticed she was also tugging self-consciously at her top. "We're here to get bendy and zen. Or whatever it is yoga people do."

Before Rosie could respond, a willowy young woman with a serene smile glided to the front of the room.

"Namaste, everyone," she said in a voice as smooth as honey. "I'm Serenity, and I'll be guiding your practice today."

Emma snorted quietly. "Serenity? Bet that's not what's on her birth certificate."

"Shh," Lisa elbowed her, but Rosie could see the corners of her mouth twitching. "Let's begin in a comfortable seated position," Serenity instructed, folding herself effortlessly into a cross-legged pose.

Rosie lowered herself to her mat, wincing as her knees

creaked in protest. Comfortable? Ha! She hadn't sat cross-legged since primary school.

"Now, close your eyes and focus on your breath," Serenity continued, her voice taking on a dreamy quality. "Inhale positivity, exhale negativity."

Rosie tried to focus, she really did. But all she could think about was whether her muffin top was visible to the entire class.

"Psst," Catherine whispered from her left. "Is it normal for my foot to be going numb?"

Before Rosie could answer, Serenity's voice cut through the room. "And now, let's move into our first pose. We'll start with a simple Cat-Cow stretch." Simple. Right. Rosie watched in growing alarm as Serenity demonstrated, her spine undulating with feline grace.

Around the room, bodies began to move in sync, a sea of arching backs and tucked chins. "Come on, ladies," Emma muttered. "If that slip of a girl can do it, so can we." Rosie positioned herself on her hands and knees, feeling ridiculous. She arched her back, trying to mimic Serenity's fluid movements. A strangled yelp from her right made her turn her head. Julie, in her enthusiasm, had arched her back so dramatically she'd lost her balance and face-planted onto her mat.

"I'm okay," Julie whispered, her voice muffled by the mat. "Just... checking the thread count on this thing."

Rosie bit her lip to keep from laughing out loud. She chanced a glance at the others. Lisa, ever the perfectionist, was frowning in concentration as she moved between poses. Catherine looked like she was trying to impersonate a startled cat, her movements jerky and uncertain. And Emma... well, Emma appeared to be doing her own thing entirely.

"Beautiful, everyone," Serenity called out, her eyes suspiciously avoiding their corner of the room. "Now, let's move into Downward Facing Dog."

Oh, good grief.

Rosie watched in mounting horror as Serenity demonstrated, her lithe body forming a perfect inverted V. Around the room, participants followed suit, a forest of spandex-clad bottoms rising into the air.

"You've got to be kidding me," Emma muttered, but gamely began to push herself up. Rosie took a deep breath and attempted to mimic the pose. Immediately, she felt the blood rushing to her head. Her hamstrings screamed in protest, and she was pretty sure her yoga pants were giving everyone behind her a view they hadn't signed up for.

"Breathe into the pose," Serenity instructed, gliding between mats. "Feel your spine lengthening, your shoulders opening."

All Rosie could feel was an overwhelming urge to collapse onto her mat and never move again. A muffled whimper from Catherine caught her attention. Rosie turned her head, no easy feat in her current position, to see her friend frozen in place, her arms shaking with effort.

"I'm stuck," Catherine whispered, panic evident in her voice. "I can't move. Oh god, I'm going to be in this position forever."

Rosie bit her lip, torn between concern for her friend and an almost overwhelming urge to burst out laughing. The sight of Catherine, bottom in the air, face a mask of wide-eyed panic, was almost too much to bear.

"Hold on," Lisa whispered, attempting to shimmy over to Catherine without breaking her pose. "I'll help you down."

What followed was a comedy of errors that would have put the Three Stooges to shame. Lisa, in her attempt to assist Catherine, lost her balance and toppled sideways, taking Emma down with her. Emma, flailing wildly, kicked out and caught Julie's ankle, sending her sprawling across her mat with a yelp. Rosie, distracted by the domino effect of falling friends, felt her arms give way. She collapsed onto her mat with an undignified "oof," rolling onto her back just in time to see Catherine slowly topple over like a felled tree.

For a moment, there was silence. Then, from the tangle of limbs and yoga mats, Emma's voice rose in a barely suppressed giggle. "Well, that's one way to get unstuck." It was as if a dam had burst. Laughter erupted from their corner of the room, loud and unrestrained.

Rosie felt tears streaming down her face as she gasped for breath, each glance at her friends setting off a fresh wave of giggles.

"Ladies," Serenity's voice cut through their mirth, her serene tone now decidedly frosty. "Perhaps this isn't the right class for you."

Rosie looked up to see Serenity looming over them, her perfect posture somehow managing to convey extreme disapproval. Around the room, other participants were twisted in impossible poses, staring at them with a mixture of annoyance and pity.

"You know what?" Emma said, pushing herself to her feet with as much dignity as she could muster. "I think you might be right. This isn't the place for us at all."

One by one, they gathered their mats and belongings, still fighting back giggles. As they filed out of the studio, Rosie could have sworn she heard a collective sigh of relief from the remaining participants.

Once outside, they looked at each other, dishevelled and red-faced.

"Oh my god," Julie gasped, wiping tears from her eyes. "Did you see Serenity's face? I thought she was going to spontaneously combust from all that repressed rage."

"Forget Serenity," Lisa chuckled. "Did you see Catherine? I

thought we were going to have to call the fire brigade to get you down!"

Catherine, far from being offended, was laughing harder than any of them. "I haven't been that flexible since... well, ever! I think I discovered muscles I didn't even know I had."

As their laughter subsided, Rosie looked at her watch. It was barely midday. "Well, ladies," she said, a mischievous glint in her eye. "It's five o'clock somewhere. Who's for a glass of wine?" A chorus of enthusiastic agreement met her suggestion. Twenty minutes later, they were ensconced in a cozy booth at The Red Lion, still in their yoga gear, a bottle of Pinot Grigio chilling in an ice bucket before them.

"To the Sensational Sixties Squad," Emma proclaimed, raising her glass. "May all our adventures be as memorable as this one."

"And may we never attempt the Downward Facing Dog again," Catherine added, clinking her glass against Emma's. As they sipped their wine, recounting the morning's mishaps with increasing embellishment, Rosie looked around at these women - Emma with her irreverent humour, Lisa with her quiet strength, Julie with her artistic spirit, and Catherine with her newfound willingness to laugh at herself - and felt profoundly grateful.

"You know," she said, during a lull in the conversation, "I haven't laughed like that in years. I'd forgotten how good it feels."

The others nodded in agreement, their faces softening with understanding. "It's easy to forget, isn't it?" Julie mused. "When you're caught up in the day-to-day grind, dealing with life's... challenges."

She didn't need to elaborate. They all knew she was referring to her separation from Tom.

"Well, I for one refuse to forget again," Emma declared, pouring herself another glass of wine. "Life's too short to take ourselves so seriously. We're not dead yet, ladies. Far from it."

"Yes," Lisa agreed. "So, what's next on our adventure list? Skydiving? Burlesque dancing? Tattoos?"

Catherine nearly choked on her wine. "Let's not get carried away," she spluttered. "Maybe we could start with something a bit less... extreme? Like a cooking class?"

"Ooh, yes!" Julie's eyes lit up. "I've always wanted to learn how to make proper French pastries."

As they debated the merits of potential adventures, Rosie sat back and simply basked in the moment. Who would have thought that a disastrous yoga class would lead to this? She caught her reflection in the pub's mirror and barely recognised herself. Her hair was a mess, her face flushed with laughter and wine, and her yoga outfit was decidedly worse for wear. But her eyes were sparkling with a light that had been missing for far too long.

"Penny for your thoughts?" Lisa asked, nudging Rosie gently. Rosie smiled, raising her glass. "I was just thinking... here's to new beginnings. And to friends who make those beginnings worth celebrating."

GIRLS' NIGHT OUT

Rosie stood with her hands on hips, surveying the battlefield of discarded outfits strewn across her bed. Who knew deciding what to wear for a night out could be so stressful? It had been years since she'd gone to a pub for anything other than a quiet Sunday lunch. Her phone buzzed with a message from Emma:

"If you're not wearing something that would make your ex-husband's eyes pop out, you're doing it wrong."

Rosie chuckled, shaking her head. Trust Emma to cut right to the chase. With renewed determination, she pushed aside the sensible blouses and reached for a sparkly top she'd bought on impulse years ago but never had the courage to wear.

"Well," she muttered to her reflection as she slipped it on, "if not now, when?"

An hour later, Rosie found herself outside The Golden Fleece, the local pub that had recently undergone a trendy renovation. Gone were the dartboards and dusty horse brasses; in their place were exposed brick walls and Edison bulbs dangling from the ceiling. She spotted her friends huddled near the entrance, looking like a group of teenagers on their first night out - if teenagers had wrinkles and creaky joints.

"Well, well, well," Emma whistled as Rosie approached. "Look who decided to bring the disco ball with her."

Rosie felt her cheeks warm. "Is it too much? I knew I should have gone with the cardigan..."

"Don't you dare," Lisa interjected, giving Rosie an approving once-over. "You look fantastic. We all do. Right, ladies?"

There was a chorus of agreement, though Catherine still looked like she might bolt at any moment. Her usual conservative attire had been replaced by a flowing bohemian top that Julie had clearly had a hand in choosing.

"Right then," Emma said, rubbing her hands together with glee. "Let's go paint this town red!"

As they entered the pub, Rosie was struck by how loud it was. The place was packed, mostly with people half their age, all shouting to be heard over the thumping music.

"Good grief," Julie yelled, her eyes wide. "Is this what pubs are like now? I feel like I've stepped into a nightclub!"

"What?" Lisa shouted back, cupping her ear.

"I said... oh, never mind. Let's find a table!"

They managed to snag a booth in the corner, squeezing in together like sardines in a sparkly tin. A young waiter approached, his eyes widening slightly at the sight of them.

"What can I get you... ladies?" he asked, his tone suggesting he wasn't quite sure if that was the right form of address.

"Gin and tonic," Emma said promptly. "And keep 'em coming, sonny. We've got a lot of lost time to make up for."

The others placed their orders - a vodka martini for Lisa, white wine for Julie, a rather daring cosmopolitan for Catherine, and after a moment's hesitation, a mojito for

Rosie. As the waiter walked away, looking slightly shell-shocked, Rosie leaned in.

"I've never had a mojito before," she confessed. "I'm not even sure what's in it."

"Rum, mint, and a healthy dose of midlife crisis," Emma quipped. "You'll love it."

Their drinks arrived, and Rosie took a tentative sip of her mojito. The fresh, minty flavour with a kick of rum was a revelation. "Oh my," she said, her eyebrows rising. "That's rather good."

"Told you," Emma grinned, raising her gin and tonic in a toast. "To the Sensational Sixties Squad and our first big night out!"

They clinked glasses, giggling like schoolgirls. As the alcohol began to work its magic, their inhibitions started to loosen.

Lisa, usually so composed, was regaling them with increasingly hilarious stories from her life in politics. "...and then," she gasped, wiping tears of laughter from her eyes, "the CEO walked in, wearing nothing but his boxer shorts and a tie!"

The table erupted in laughter, drawing curious glances from nearby patrons. Rosie couldn't remember the last time she'd laughed so hard.

"Ladies, ladies," Emma said, holding up her hand. "I hate to interrupt, but nature calls. Anyone care to join me in powdering our noses?"

Catherine and Julie volunteered to accompany her, leaving Rosie and Lisa at the table.

"Having fun?" Lisa asked, giving Rosie a warm smile. Rosie nodded enthusiastically.

"More than I've had in years. I'd forgotten what it was like to just... let loose."

"I know what you mean," Lisa agreed. "It's like we've been

given permission to be silly again. To remember who we were before life got so..."

"Complicated?" Rosie finished for her.

"Exactly."

Their conversation was interrupted by a commotion near the bar. Rosie turned to see Emma engaged in what appeared to be a heated debate with a group of young men.

"Oh lord," Lisa muttered. "What's she up to now?"

As they watched, Emma gestured dramatically, nearly knocking over someone's drink in the process. The young men were laughing, but not unkindly. In fact, they seemed to be thoroughly entertained by whatever Emma was saying.

"Should we rescue her?" Rosie asked, half-rising from her seat. Lisa shook her head, a knowing smile on her face. "Trust me, Emma doesn't need rescuing. I'd be more worried about those poor boys."

Sure enough, a moment later, Emma returned to the table, a triumphant grin on her face and a fresh drink in her hand.

"Gentlemen…" she announced, "are not dead. Those lovely lads just bought me a drink and invited us to join their pub quiz team."

"Their what?" Catherine squeaked, looking alarmed.

"Pub quiz, darling. You know, trivia? Come on, it'll be fun!"

Before they knew it, they found themselves squeezed around a large table with a group of young men, all of whom seemed both amused and slightly in awe of their new teammates.

"Right," said one of the lads, a fresh-faced young man who introduced himself as Tom. "We've got sports, pop culture, history, and science. What are your strong suits, ladies?"

Emma puffed out her chest. "I'll have you know I'm a walking encyclopaedia of 60s and 70s music trivia."

"Perfect," Tom grinned. "And the rest of you?"

To everyone's surprise, it was Catherine who spoke up next. "I... I'm quite good at history. Especially British monarchs."

"Brilliant! Lisa, what about you?"

Lisa straightened her shoulders. "Put me down for politics and current events. I may be semi-retired, but I still read the Financial Times every morning."

Julie raised her hand. "I can handle the art questions. And possibly literature."

All eyes turned to Rosie. She felt a moment of panic. What was she good at? She'd spent so many years being Derek's wife, Mary's mother, that she'd almost forgotten what her own interests were.

"I... I suppose I know a bit about gardening," she said hesitantly. "And I'm not bad at general knowledge."

"Sounds like we've got all our bases covered then," Tom said enthusiastically. "Are you going to show us youngsters how it's done?"

As the quiz got underway, Rosie was caught up in the excitement. She surprised herself by knowing answers to questions she didn't even realise she knew. The years fell away as she and her friends laughed, debated, and celebrated each correct answer.

It was during a break between rounds that Rosie noticed him. A distinguished-looking man at the bar, his salt-and-pepper hair neatly trimmed, a glass of whiskey in his hand. He caught her eye and smiled, raising his glass in a small salute. Rosie felt a flutter in her stomach that she hadn't experienced in years. She smiled back, then quickly looked away, her cheeks warming.

"Well, well," Emma's voice came from beside her, full of mischief. "What have we here? Has our Rosie spotted a silver fox?"

"I don't know what you're talking about," Rosie muttered, but she could feel her blush deepening.

"Oh yes, you do," Emma grinned. "Go on, go talk to him. We'll cover for you in the next round."

"I couldn't possibly..." Rosie began, but Emma was already gently pushing her out of her seat.

"You can, and you will. Doctor's orders."

"Doctor?" Rosie asked, confused. Emma nodded towards the man at the bar. "That's Mike Thompson. He's a GP at the local surgery. Divorced, no kids, and if the local gossip is to be believed, an excellent dancer. Now go!"

Before Rosie could protest further, she found herself standing and making her way to the bar. Her heart was pounding so loudly that she was sure everyone could hear it.

"Hello," she said, wincing internally at how breathless she sounded. "I'm Rosie."

Mike turned to her, his smile widening. "Hello, Rosie. I'm Mike. Can I buy you a drink?"

His voice was deep and warm, with a hint of a Scottish burr. "That would be lovely, thank you."

As Mike ordered her another mojito, Rosie caught sight of her friends at the quiz table. They were all giving her enthusiastic thumbs up, with Emma miming what appeared to be a very inappropriate gesture.

Rosie turned back to Mike, determined to make conversation. "So, you're a doctor?"

Mike nodded. "GP, yes. Though tonight I'm off duty and strictly here for the pub quiz. Which I see you've already been recruited for."

Rosie laughed. "Yes, though I'm not sure how much help I'm being. It's been a while since I've done anything like this."

"Well, from what I could see, you were holding your own quite well," Mike said, his eyes twinkling. "Especially on that last gardening question. I was impressed."

They fell into easy conversation, discussing everything from the merits of different rose varieties to the challenges of modern healthcare. Rosie was surprised at how comfortable she felt, and how easily the words flowed. It was only when she heard a commotion from the quiz table that she realised how much time had passed. She turned to see Emma engaged in what appeared to be a heated debate with the quiz master.

"Oh dear," Rosie muttered. "I should probably..."

Mike nodded understandingly. "Go rescue your friends. But Rosie..." he hesitated for a moment. "I've enjoyed talking with you. Perhaps we could do it again sometime? Over dinner, maybe?"

Rosie felt a thrill run through her. Was she being asked out on a date? At her age? She found herself nodding before she could overthink it. "I'd like that very much."

As she made her way back to the table, she could hear Emma's voice rising above the general hubbub. "...and I'm telling you, it was Mick Jagger, not Keith Richards!"

The quiz master, a harried-looking young man, was shaking his head. "I'm sorry, madam, but the answer sheet clearly states..."

"Oh, stuff your answer sheet," Emma interrupted. "I was there, sonny. Front row at Hyde Park. Trust me, I know my Rolling Stones."

Rosie slid into her seat just as Emma, frustrated by the quiz master's intransigence, pulled out a packet of cigarettes and a lighter. "Emma, no!" Lisa hissed. "You can't smoke in here. It's been banned for years!"

But Emma, fuelled by alcohol and indignation, wasn't listening. She stuck a cigarette between her lips and flicked the lighter. What happened next seemed to unfold in slow motion. The sprinkler system, detecting the flame, suddenly burst into life. Water rained down on the entire pub, soaking patrons, short-circuiting the sound system, and turning the quiz sheets into soggy pulp.

For a moment, there was stunned silence. Then, as if on cue, the entire pub erupted into chaos. People shrieked, slipping and sliding on the wet floor as they made for the exits.

Rosie looked at her friends, all of them dripping wet, mascara running down their faces.

"I wasn't going to actually smoke it. I only lit it to annoy the questionmaster. Damn."

As they stumbled out of the pub, Rosie caught Mike's eye across the street. He was as soaked as the rest of them, but he was grinning and gave her a wink that made her heart skip a beat.

"Well, ladies," Emma said, wringing water out of her hair, "I'd say our first big night out was a roaring success, wouldn't you? I "didn't let myself down one bit."

And as they linked arms and began the wobbly walk home, already planning their next adventure, Rosie couldn't help but agree. It had been chaotic, slightly ridiculous, and utterly, wonderfully perfect.

DATE NIGHT JITTERS

She'd had her roots done, but not her nails, eyebrows or eyelashes. Should she have? Should she have waxed her legs and her bikini line? And her chin? And the moustache that was starting to appear above her lip?

How much effort did people put into dating these days?

The last time she'd been on a first date, Margaret Thatcher had been in office and shoulder pads were considered the height of fashion.

"It's just dinner," she muttered to herself, pushing aside a series of cardigans that suddenly seemed to mock her with their sensibleness. "With a handsome doctor. Who you barely know. At your age. Oh, good grief."

Her phone buzzed, making her jump. A message from Emma flashed on the screen: "Operation Silver Fox is go! We'll be there in 10 with reinforcements. Don't you dare get dressed without us!"

Rosie felt a mix of relief and trepidation. On one hand, she desperately needed help. On the other... well, letting the Sensational Sixties Squad loose in her bedroom seemed like a recipe for chaos.

True to Emma's word, precisely ten minutes later, the doorbell rang. Rosie opened it to find her friends on the doorstep, armed with what appeared to be enough beauty supplies to stock a small salon. "Right," Emma said, brushing past Rosie with determination. "Where's the patient? We have a severe case of first-date jitters to cure."

"I'm not sure 'patient' is the right word," Rosie protested weakly, but she was already being steered towards her bedroom by Lisa and Julie.

"Nonsense," Lisa said briskly. "You're in need of emergency intervention, and we're your style paramedics."

Catherine brought up the rear, looking slightly overwhelmed by the rapid-fire chatter of the others. "I brought wine," she said, holding up a bottle like a peace offering. "I thought we might need it."

As they piled into Rosie's bedroom, Emma immediately made a beeline for the wardrobe. "Right, let's see what we're working with here... oh my. Rosie, darling, when was the last time you bought something that wasn't beige?"

Rosie felt her cheeks warm. "They are my pre-sensational Sixties clothes. I've got lots of colourful clothes in there." Rosie opened a small wardrobe and the sight of colours and patterns aplenty caused gasps from her friends.

"This is more like it. What on earth possessed you to buy so many clothes in beige?"

"It's stylish," replied Rosie.

"For a carpet, maybe," Emma retorted. "Aha! Now this has potential." She held up a deep green wrap dress that Rosie had forgotten she owned. It had been an impulse buy years ago, worn once to a Christmas party and then relegated to the back of the wardrobe.

"I can't wear that," Rosie said, eyeing the dress dubiously. "It's too... young."

"Nonsense," Lisa interjected, taking the dress from Emma

and holding it up to Rosie. "It's classic. Timeless. And it'll bring out the colour of your eyes beautifully."

"But..." Rosie began, only to be cut off by Julie.

"No buts," Julie said firmly. "Trust us, Rosie. Mike won't know what hit him."

As Rosie reluctantly tried on the dress, Catherine busied herself pouring generous glasses of wine for everyone.

"Dutch courage," she said with a wink, handing Rosie a glass.

"Now," Emma said, rubbing her hands together with glee. "Let's talk hair and makeup."

What followed was a whirlwind of activity that left Rosie feeling like she was in the eye of a very glamorous storm. Julie, with her artistic eye, took charge of makeup, wielding brushes and palettes with the precision of a master painter.

"Hold still," Julie instructed, applying eyeshadow with intense concentration. "I'm going for a smoky eye effect."

"Smoky eye?" Rosie squeaked. "Isn't that a bit much for dinner?"

"Trust the process," Julie said serenely. "You'll see."

Meanwhile, Lisa had taken on the challenge of Rosie's hair. "When was the last time you had a proper cut and colour?" she asked, frowning at Rosie's reflection in the mirror.

"Yesterday. I went to that place down the road. It was only £20." Lisa's raised eyebrow spoke volumes. "Right. We're booking you a proper appointment first thing tomorrow. But for now, we'll work with what we've got."

As Lisa began teasing and styling, Emma rummaged through Rosie's jewellery box.

"Surely you must have something here that isn't... oh, hello. What's this little beauty?"

She held up a pair of dangly earrings that Rosie had

forgotten about. They'd been a gift from Derek years ago, never worn because they seemed too flashy for everyday life.

"Perfect," Emma declared. "These will add just the right amount of sparkle."

Catherine, meanwhile, had been tasked with shoe selection. She emerged from Rosie's closet looking triumphant. "I found these," she said, holding up a pair of strappy sandals with a modest heel. "They're not too high, but they'll elongate your legs beautifully."

Rosie eyed the shoes warily. "I haven't worn heels in years," she admitted. "What if I fall flat on my face?"

"Then Mike will have a chance to show off his bedside manner," Emma quipped, earning herself a playful swat from Lisa.

As the makeover progressed, fuelled by wine and increasingly outrageous stories of past dating disasters, Rosie's nerves began to settle. The laughter and camaraderie of her friends were infectious, reminding her that no matter what happened on this date, she had a support system to fall back on.

Finally, after what felt like hours of primping and polishing, Emma declared the transformation complete.

"Ladies," she said with a flourish, "I give you the new and improved Rosie!"

Rosie turned to look in the full-length mirror and gasped. The woman staring back at her was her, but somehow way more than her. The green dress hugged her curves in all the right places, the subtle makeup enhanced her features without overwhelming them, and her hair fell in soft waves around her face.

"Oh my," she breathed, turning this way and that. "Is that really me?"

"That," Lisa said with satisfaction, "is the real you. The you that's always been there, just waiting for the right moment to shine."

Rosie felt tears prick in her eyes. "Thank you," she said, turning to embrace each of her friends in turn. "I couldn't have done this without you."

"Of course you couldn't," Emma said briskly, but her eyes were suspiciously bright. "Now, no crying! You'll ruin Julie's masterpiece."

Just then, the doorbell rang, making them all jump.

"He's early!" Rosie yelped, suddenly panicking again. "Oh god, I'm not ready. I can't do this. What was I thinking?"

"Deep breaths," Lisa instructed, gripping Rosie by the shoulders. "You can do this. You're gorgeous, you're intelligent, and you're going to knock his socks off."

"But what if I say something stupid?" Rosie fretted. "What if I use the wrong fork? What if--" Her spiral of worst-case scenarios was cut off by Emma, who thrust a small flask into her hand. "Emergency backup," she said with a wink. "Just in case."

Before Rosie could protest, she was being ushered down the stairs, her friends following like a very enthusiastic honour guard.

"Remember," Julie called as Rosie reached for the door handle. "You're not just Rosie tonight. You're Rosie 2.0 - sassy, confident, and ready for adventure!"

With one last deep breath, Rosie opened the door. Mike stood on the doorstep, looking devastatingly handsome in a well-cut suit. His eyes widened appreciatively as he took in Rosie's appearance. "Wow," he said, a slow smile spreading across his face. "You look... amazing."

Rosie felt a blush creep up her cheeks. "Thank you," she managed. "You look very nice too."

There was a moment of awkward silence, broken by a

not-so-subtle cough from behind Rosie. She turned to see her friends attempting (and failing) to look inconspicuous.

"Oh! Um, these are my friends," Rosie said, gesturing vaguely behind her. "They were just... helping me get ready."

Mike's smile widened as he waved to the group. "Hello, ladies. Thanks for taking such good care of Rosie. I promise to have her home by midnight."

"Make it one!" Emma called out, earning herself an elbow in the ribs from Lisa. As Mike offered Rosie his arm and led her to his car, she could hear the excited chatter of her friends behind her.

The drive to the restaurant was filled with light conversation, punctuated by moments of comfortable silence. Rosie felt very relaxed, Mike's gentle manner putting her at ease.

As they were seated at their table, Rosie's earlier panic about using the wrong fork resurfaced. She eyed the array of cutlery before her with trepidation. Mike, noticing her hesitation, leaned in conspiratorially.

"I'll let you in on a secret," he said in a low voice. "I never know which fork to use either. I just start from the outside and work my way in."

Rosie laughed, feeling the last of her tension melt away.

"And I thought doctors were supposed to know everything."

"Certainly not," said Mike with a wink. "We're just very good at faking it when we don't."

As the evening progressed, Rosie found herself thoroughly enjoying Mike's company. He was intelligent, witty, and a great listener. They swapped stories about their careers, their families, and the joys and challenges of starting over in their sixties.

"I have to admit," Mike said as they lingered over dessert, "I was a bit nervous about tonight."

Rosie raised an eyebrow. "You? Nervous? But you seem so confident."

Mike chuckled. "Well, as I said, doctors are very good at faking it. But the truth is, it's been a long time since I've been on a first date. And when I saw you in the pub that night... well, let's just say you made quite an impression."

Rosie felt a warm glow spread through her.

"Even with the impromptu shower courtesy of the sprinkler system?"

"Especially then," Mike said, his eyes twinkling. "Any woman who can laugh in the face of disaster is someone I want to get to know better."

As they left the restaurant, Rosie felt a flutter of anticipation in her stomach. The night had gone better than she could have hoped, but now came the moment of truth - the end-of-date goodbye.

They walked slowly to Rosie's front door, neither seeming in a hurry for the evening to end.

"I had a wonderful time tonight, Rosie," Mike said as they reached her doorstep.

"So did I," Rosie replied, suddenly feeling shy. "Thank you for a lovely evening."

There was a moment of charged silence, both of them unsure of how to proceed. Then, almost simultaneously, they both leaned in. The kiss was sweet, a little awkward, but filled with promise. As they pulled apart, Rosie felt a girlish giggle bubble up inside her.

"What's so funny?" Mike asked, looking amused. Rosie shook her head, still smiling.

"Nothing. It's just... I feel like a teenager again. In a good way."

Mike's smile widened. "Me too. Listen, Rosie... I'd like to see you again. If you're interested, that is."

"I'd like that very much," Rosie said, surprised at how easily the words came.

As Mike walked back to his car, Rosie let herself into the house, her heart light and her cheeks hurting from smiling. She kicked off her shoes and was about to head upstairs when she noticed a light on in the living room.

Curious, she peeked in - and found all four of her friends sprawled across her furniture, fast asleep. Empty wine glasses and snack bowls littered the coffee table, and Emma was snoring softly, a fashion magazine draped across her face.

Rosie felt a rush of affection for these women who had quite literally waited up for her. She tiptoed over to the hall closet and pulled out a stack of blankets, gently draping one over each of her sleeping friends.

Then she turned out the light and headed up to bed. How lovely was this? A date with a handsome doctor and friends who waited for her to get home.

A few months ago, she'd been feeling lost and alone. Now, she had a group of amazing friends, a potential new romance, and a sense of excitement about the future that she hadn't felt in years.

"Sixty and just getting started," she murmured to herself as she climbed into bed. "Who would have thought?"

With a contented sigh, Rosie drifted off to sleep, already looking forward to sharing every detail of her date with her friends in the morning.

"MORNING AFTER MUSINGS"

The early morning sunlight filtered through Rosie's bedroom curtains, gently rousing her from a night of pleasant dreams. As consciousness slowly returned, so did the memories of the previous evening.

Mike's charming smile, the warmth of his hand on hers, that sweet, slightly awkward goodnight kiss... Rosie felt a girlish giggle bubble up inside her, and she pressed her face into her pillow to muffle it.

At 63, she shouldn't be feeling like a teenager with a crush. And yet...

Throwing on her dressing gown, Rosie made her way downstairs, following the enticing aroma of bacon.

In the kitchen, she found a scene of cheerful chaos. Emma, still glamorous despite her slightly crumpled clothes, was at the stove, wielding a spatula like a conductor's baton.

"The key to perfect bacon," she was saying, "is to let it dance in the pan. A little sizzle here, a little pop there..."

Lisa and Julie were setting the table, playfully arguing over the proper placement of napkins, while Catherine was juicing oranges with the focused determination of a chemist working on a crucial experiment.

"Good morning, ladies," Rosie said, unable to keep the smile from her voice. Four heads whipped around, and Rosie was engulfed in a group hug that threatened to squeeze the breath out of her. "There she is!" Emma crowed. "Our Cinderella, returned from the ball!"

"More like returned from a very nice dinner," Rosie corrected, extricating herself from the tangle of arms. "And shouldn't I be the one making you breakfast? You're my guests, after all."

"Nonsense," Catherine said firmly, pressing a glass of fresh orange juice into Rosie's hand. "Consider this our thank you for the impromptu slumber party."

"Although next time," Lisa added, rubbing her neck, "perhaps we could upgrade from 'passed out on the sofa' to 'actual beds'?"

Rosie laughed. "Deal. Now, is anyone going to ask about my date, or are you all just going to pretend you're not dying to know?"

There was a moment of silence before the kitchen erupted into a cacophony of questions.

"Was he a gentleman?"

"Did he use the right fork?"

"How was the goodnight kiss?"

"Is he as handsome up close as he is from afar?"

"Ladies, ladies," Emma interrupted, brandishing her spatula like a gavel. "Let the woman breathe. And more importantly, let her eat. We'll conduct this interrogation properly, over bacon sandwiches and coffee."

Soon, they were all settled around Rosie's kitchen table, plates piled high with Emma's "dancing bacon" sandwiches and mugs of steaming coffee at the ready.

"Right," Emma said, leaning forward with the air of a

general planning a military campaign. "Start at the beginning and don't leave out a single detail."

Rosie took a sip of coffee to hide her smile. "Well, he arrived precisely on time..." As Rosie recounted the events of the evening, her friends listened with rapt attention, interjecting with gasps, giggles, and the occasional sage nod.

"He got all your jokes?" Julie said, impressed. "Even the one about the vicar and the llama?" Rosie nodded. "And he even added his own punchline!"

"Oh, he's a keeper," Lisa declared. "A man with a good sense of humour is worth his weight in gold."

"And how about his table manners?" Catherine inquired. "No unfortunate incidents with escargot or oversized mouthfuls?"

"Perfect gentleman," Rosie assured her. "Though I must admit, I was so nervous about using the wrong fork that I barely noticed what he was doing!"

"Forget the forks," Emma cut in impatiently. "Tell us about the kiss!"

Rosie felt herself blushing. "Emma! A lady doesn't kiss and tell."

"Nonsense," Emma scoffed. "That's exactly what ladies do. Now spill!"

Rosie sighed in mock exasperation, but her eyes were twinkling. "Well, if you must know... it was lovely. Sweet, a little awkward, but... nice. Very nice."

Her friends exchanged knowing glances.

"Our Rosie's got stars in her eyes," Lisa teased gently.

"Oh, hush," Rosie said, but she couldn't keep the smile from her face. "It was just one date."

"One date will lead to another," Emma pointed out. "You did agree to see him again, didn't you?"

Rosie nodded. "We're having lunch next week."

This announcement was met with a chorus of delighted

squeals that would have put a group of teenage girls to shame.

"Right," Emma said, clapping her hands together. "We need to plan your outfit. Something casual but elegant. And we simply must do something about your hair."

"What's wrong with my hair?" Rosie asked, self-consciously patting her head.

"Nothing a good cut and colour won't fix," Lisa said diplomatically. "I know just the place. They work miracles."

As her friends began to plan her makeover with the enthusiasm of fairy godmothers preparing Cinderella for the ball, Rosie felt a warmth spread through her chest that had nothing to do with the coffee.

"Earth to Rosie," Julie's voice broke through her reverie. "You've got that dreamy look again. Thinking about Doctor Charming?"

Rosie shook her head, smiling. "No. I was thinking about how lucky I am to have friends like you."

There was a moment of silence as her words sank in, and then Rosie found herself engulfed in another group hug, this one gentler but no less heartfelt.

"Oh, darling," Emma said. "We're the lucky ones. Now, let's clean up this kitchen and hit the shops. We've got a second date to prepare for!"

As they bustled about, clearing plates and wiping down surfaces, the kitchen filled with chatter and laughter. Plans were made for shopping trips, spa days, and future group outings.

Rosie's date with Mike had been wonderful, but this - this warm, chaotic, joy-filled morning with her friends - was, in its way, even better.

"You OK?" asked Catherine, noticing how deep in thought her friend was.

"Yes. Just thinking... sixty and just getting started. Who would have thought?"

Catherine squeezed her shoulder. "Oh, I think we all had an inkling. You just needed a little push."

"More like a shove," Emma called from the doorway. "Now come on, you two! The shops await, and we have a second-date outfit to find!"

THE AFFAIR NEXT DOOR

*R*osie hummed to herself as she watered the geraniums on her windowsill, a spring in her step that hadn't been there a few weeks ago. The memory of her date with Mike still brought a smile to her face, and she found herself looking forward to their next outing with excitement and nervous anticipation.

The doorbell's chime interrupted her reverie. Wiping her hands on her apron, Rosie hurried to answer it, finding Emma on her doorstep, practically bouncing enthusiastically.

"Get your walking shoes on, Red," Emma announced without preamble. "We're going for a stroll in the park, and I've got a surprise for you."

Rosie raised an eyebrow. "A surprise? Should I be worried?"

Emma's grin widened. "Only if you're allergic to making new friends. Come on, the others are waiting!"

Curiosity piqued, Rosie quickly changed into more suitable attire and followed Emma out the door. She spotted Lisa, Julie, and Catherine waiting for them as they approached the park entrance. But there were two unfamiliar faces as well – both women who looked to be around their age.

"Rosie!" Lisa called out, waving them over. "Come meet our new recruits!"

As they drew closer, Rosie took in the appearance of the newcomers.

"I'm Maria. Hello," one of them said, nervously. She was a petite brunette with a warm smile and a pixie haircut. She wore an immaculate white blouse and jeans with a crease in the front as if they'd been ironed repeatedly.

Rosie would soon learn that the former corporate secretary's need for order was legendary among her friends.

The other was a tall, statuesque woman with salt-and-pepper hair. Her outfit was more casual but unmistakably expensive.

"Rosie, meet Maria and Trisha," Julie said, gesturing to each woman in turn. "They're my neighbours from down the street, and they've decided to join our merry band of mischief-makers. Unfortunately, they're both married, so they can't indulge in our love of gigilos and toy boys…"

"And doctors," added Emma.

Rosie felt herself blush like a schoolgirl.

"I hope you don't mind us crashing your group," said Maria. "Julie's been telling us all about your adventures, and well… it sounded like fun."

Trisha, the taller woman, grinned and added, "What Maria means is, we're desperately in need of some excitement in our lives, and you lot seem to attract it like magnets."

Rosie laughed, immediately warming to the new additions. "Well, you've certainly come to the right place. Though I can't promise all our adventures will be entirely dignified."

"Dignity is overrated," Emma declared, linking arms with Maria and Trisha. "Now, let's get this walk started. I've got gossip to share, and my tongue is practically itching with the effort of keeping it to myself."

As they set off down the park's winding paths, Rosie found herself falling into step beside Maria

"Julie mentioned you live down the street. Have you been in the neighbourhood long?"

Maria nodded, her perfectly styled hair barely moving. "Oh yes, David – that's my husband – and I have been here for nearly twenty years now. It's a lovely area, isn't it?"

"It is," Rosie agreed. "Though I must admit, I've only recently started to appreciate it again. Funny how a change in perspective can make familiar surroundings seem new."

A shadow passed over Maria's face, so quickly Rosie almost missed it.

"Yes, I suppose that's true," she said softly. "David always says I'm too..." she trailed off, that shadow passing over her face again.

Trisha, who had been quiet up until now, suddenly spoke up. "Too what, Maria? Too fun? Too happy? Because if that's what David thinks, then David can go take a long walk off a short pier."

The vehemence in Trisha's tone took Rosie by surprise. There was clearly some history here that she wasn't privy to.

Maria flushed, looking uncomfortable. "It's not like that, Trish. David just... he likes things to be a certain way. Orderly, you know?"

"And by 'orderly,' you mean 'boring as watching paint dry,'" Trisha muttered but subsided when Lisa shot her a warning look.

As they strolled along, Rosie chatted with Trisha, who turned out to have a wicked sense of humour and a wealth of stories from her days running a successful event-planning business with her husband, John.

"It's all about the details," Trisha was saying, gesturing

expansively. "You wouldn't believe the things people want at their weddings these days.

"Last month, we had a couple who insisted on having live butterflies released during their vows. Can you imagine? The poor vicar nearly had a heart attack when one landed on his nose mid-sermon!"

Rosie was laughed at Trisha's impression of the flustered vicar when she heard a sharp intake of breath from beside her. She turned to see Maria frozen in place, her face drained of colour.

"Maria? What's wrong?" Rosie asked, concerned. But Maria didn't seem to hear her. Her gaze was fixed on something across the park. Rosie followed her line of sight. On a bench partially hidden by a large oak tree, sat a man with a young woman– easily half his age – perched beside him, laughing at something he'd said.

"Do you know her?" asked Rosie. "No, but I know him," said Maria. "He's an absolute scumbag."

As they watched, the man reached out and tucked a strand of hair behind the woman's ear, his hand lingering on her cheek in an unmistakably intimate gesture.

"Oh, shit," Emma muttered, having noticed the scene as well. For a moment, no one moved. Then, without a word, Maria turned on her heel and began walking rapidly in the opposite direction.

"Maria, wait!" Lisa called, but Maria didn't slow down. The group exchanged helpless glances before Trisha took charge.

"Right," she said briskly. "Julie and Catherine – you go after Maria. Make sure she's okay. The rest of us need to have a little chat."

As Julie and Catherine hurried after Maria, Trisha turned to the remaining women, her expression grim.

"Well, ladies, it seems we have a situation on our hands. I'm going over to talk to that scum bag."

"What's going on?" asked Rosie. "I'm confused."

"That two-timing, snake-in-the-grass, sorry excuse for a man is Maria's husband," Emma fumed, her hands clenched into fists.

"Oh no," said Rosie, genuinely shocked.

"I'm going over there and give him a piece of my mind," said Emma, "turning on her heels and beginning to march towards the bench.

"Do you think... is it possible there's an innocent explanation? Maybe that woman is a relative or a colleague..." said Rosie.

Trisha shook her head, her expression sad. "I wish I could say yes, but... this isn't the first time I've had suspicions about David. He's always been a bit too friendly with his young female 'assistants,' if you know what I mean.

"Also, he treats Maria terribly. I've never liked him."

"Poor Maria," Rosie murmured. "She must be devastated."

"He's fucking gone," said Emma, returning to the group. "The scumbag must have seen us."

As the debate raged on, Rosie felt the vibration of her phone in her pocket. Fishing it out, her eyes widened as she saw the caller ID: Derek.

Her ex-husband who had an affair, prompting the collapse of their marriage, was on the phone as one of the other women was discovering that her husband was having an affair. What great timing.

For a moment, she considered ignoring the call. But something – curiosity, perhaps, or a lingering sense of obligation – made her answer.

"Hello?" she said, stepping away from the group for privacy.

"Rosie?" Derek's voice came through, sounding hesitant

and... was that a hint of vulnerability she detected? "I... I hope I'm not interrupting anything."

"No, it's fine," Rosie replied, her mind racing. "Is everything alright? Is it Mary?"

"No, no, nothing like that," Derek hastened to assure her. "Everyone's fine. I just... well, I've been doing a lot of thinking lately. About us."

"Oh?"

"I've been thinking about it for weeks, and I just... I had to call. We were good together once, weren't we? Maybe we could be again."

Rosie's thoughts were a whirlwind. Images flashed through her mind – years of shared history with Derek, the pain of their separation, the newfound joy she'd discovered with her friends, the spark of possibility with Mike. How could she possibly make sense of it all? "What are you suggesting?"

"I want us to get back together."

"Derek, you had an affair with a friend of mine."

"And I'm sorry. You have no idea how sorry I am, and how much I regret that. I adore you. I miss you. Please, Rosie. I want us to get back together."

"I... I need some time to think about this, Derek," she said finally.

"Of course," Derek replied, sounding relieved that she hadn't outright rejected the idea. "Take all the time you need. I'll be here."

As Rosie ended the call, she turned back to her friends, feeling as though the ground had shifted beneath her feet.

"Everything OK?" Emma asked.

"Yes," said Rosie. She didn't want to burden them with the conversation she'd just had.

"You look worried. What is it."

"It's nothing. Let's go and find Maria and check she's OK."

"They're in The Albion on Bridge Road. We'll meet them there."

They began to walk towards the pub. "You look miles away," said Emma.

"That was my ex-husband," said Rosie.

All eyes turned to her, concern evident on every face.

"What did he want?" Trisha asked, placing a comforting hand on her arm. Taking a deep breath, Rosie blurted out, "He wants us to get back together."

The resulting chorus of exclamations was so loud that a nearby flock of pigeons took flight in alarm.

"After everything he put you through? Oh, Rosie," Lisa said softly. "How do you feel about that?"

Rosie shook her head. "I don't know. I honestly don't know."

ACROSS TOWN, Derek sat in his sterile apartment, phone still in hand, heart racing after his call to Rosie. He gazed at the generic art on the walls, so different from the warm, lived-in feel of the home he'd shared with Rosie.

What had he been thinking? He remembered the day he'd left, convinced he was suffocating in the routines of married life. Pauline had been a spark, a chance to feel young again. But now, surrounded by the trappings of his "new life," he felt older and more lost than ever.

"You bloody fool," he muttered to himself, running a hand through his thinning hair. The excitement of his fling with Pauline had faded quickly, leaving him with nothing but regret and a deep longing for the life he'd thrown away.

He thought of Rosie, of the little things he missed – her laugh, the way she'd absentmindedly hum while reading, the comfort of simply sitting together in companionable silence. He'd mistaken that comfort for boredom, but now he recognised it for what it was – the deep, abiding love of a shared life.

Derek moved towards the window. "I have to make this right," he said to his reflection. "Somehow, I have to show Rosie that I understand now. That I want to come home."

* * *

IN THE PARK, Rosie's friends clustered around her, offering support and conflicting advice. She felt as though she were standing on the edge of a precipice. Behind her lay the familiar comfort of her life with Derek, flawed as it had been. Ahead stretched an unknown future, filled with both excitement and uncertainty. The choice, she realised, was hers to make.

"We'd all be OK if it weren't for men," said Emma, shaking her head. "Look at how much fun we all have when there are no men around to ruin things."

* * *

MIKE SAT at a corner table in the cafeteria, surrounded by his colleagues from the GP practice. The conversation flowed easily, as it always did, but Mike found his thoughts drifting to Rosie.

"Earth to Mike," chuckled Sarah, a fellow GP. "You've been staring at that coffee like it holds the secrets of the universe. What's going on in that head of yours?"

Mike looked up, a slightly sheepish grin on his face. "Sorry, just thinking about someone."

"Someone?" Tom, the youngest doctor in their group, leaned in with interest. "Don't tell me our confirmed bachelor has finally met his match?"

Mike felt a warmth creep into his cheeks. "Well, there is

this woman I've been seeing. Rosie. She's... different from anyone I've ever met."

"Do tell," Sarah encouraged, her eyes twinkling. Mike found himself talking about Rosie with an enthusiasm that surprised even him. He told them about her wit, her adventurous spirit, and the way she was embracing life in her sixties with such vigour.

"She sounds wonderful," Sarah said warmly. "But I sense there's a 'but' coming."

Mike sighed. "Her ex-husband keeps appearing in the park when she's out with her friends. I think he wants to get back with her. I know I shouldn't feel threatened, but..."

"But you do," Tom finished for him. "It's natural, Mike. You're invested in this relationship."

"Exactly," Mike nodded. "I like her. I want to be patient and give her the space to figure things out. But I can't help worrying I might lose her before we have a chance to begin."

Sarah reached out, patting his hand. "From what you've told us about Rosie, she sounds like a woman who knows her own mind. Trust in that. And in the connection you two have."

Mike smiled, feeling some of his anxiety ease. "You're right. Thanks for listening, all of you. Now, who's for another coffee? My treat."

TRUTH AND CONSEQUENCES

osie clutched her mug of tea, the porcelain warm against her palms, a stark contrast to the chill that had settled in her stomach. Around the table, the other members of the Sensational Sixties Squad sat in uncharacteristic silence, the weight of their impending task hanging heavy in the air.

Maria sat at the head of the table. Dark circles under her eyes hinted at a sleepless night, and her hands trembled slightly as she raised her cup to her lips. Rosie caught Emma's eye across the table, seeing her own uncertainty reflected back at her.

Trisha cleared her throat, breaking the tense silence. "Maria, love," she began gently, "how are you feeling this morning?"

Maria attempted a smile that didn't quite reach her eyes. "Oh, I'm fine," she said, her voice overly bright. "Just a bit of a headache. I'm sure it's nothing."

The others exchanged glances. They all knew it wasn't "nothing," but Maria's determined façade made the task ahead seem even more daunting.

Lisa leaned forward, her posture radiating calm authority. "Maria," she said softly, "I think we need to talk about what happened yesterday in the park."

Maria's smile faltered for a moment before she hitched it back into place. "Oh, that? It was silly of me to get so upset. I'm sure there's a perfectly reasonable explanation for—"

"No, Maria," Emma interrupted, her usual bluntness softened by genuine concern. "There isn't. What we saw... it wasn't innocent." The colour drained from Maria's face, her carefully constructed mask crumbling.

"You don't know that" she whispered, but there was a note of desperation in her voice.

Rosie felt her heart breaking for her friend. She reached out, covering Maria's trembling hand with her own. "Maria, we saw David with a young woman. They were... intimate."

A choked sob escaped Maria's lips, quickly stifled by her hand. "No," she shook her head vehemently. "No, you must be mistaken. David wouldn't... he couldn't... He was having a work meeting."

"I'm so sorry, Maria," Julie said. "But he wasn't. We all saw it. David was... he was behaving like a man in a relationship with this woman."

Maria's composure finally shattered. Tears streamed down her face as she curled in on herself, her body wracked with sobs. The other women moved instantly, surrounding her with comforting touches and soothing murmurs. As Rosie held Maria, offering what comfort she could, her mind drifted to her own situation. Derek's voice echoed in her memory, his words about reconciliation now tainted by the scene before her. Could she trust him again? Did she even want to?

The next few hours passed in a blur of tears, anger, and disbelief. Maria cycled through emotions like a kaleidoscope – one moment insisting there must be a mistake, the next raging against David's betrayal, then collapsing into grief again. Through it all, the Sensational Sixties Squad rallied around her.

Emma's righteous anger on Maria's behalf was tempered by Lisa's calm rationality. Catherine, drawing on her own experiences with her controlling ex, offered quiet words of understanding. Trisha, with her no-nonsense attitude, kept everyone supplied with tea, tissues, and the occasional nip of brandy "for medicinal purposes." And Rosie? She found herself in the role of silent support, her own turmoil pushed aside as she focused on being there for her friend.

The afternoon wore on, and Maria's tears subsided, leaving her looking drained but lighter, as if the weight of suspicion had been lifted, replaced by the grimmer but clearer reality of truth.

"What do I do now?" Maria asked, her voice hoarse from crying.

"You don't have to decide anything right this moment," Lisa assured her. "Take some time to process."

"But," Emma added, unable to contain herself, "when you're ready, we'll help you kick that cheating bastard to the curb."

"Emma!" Catherine admonished, but Maria let out a watery chuckle.

"It's alright," she said, managing a weak smile. "I appreciate the sentiment, even if I'm not quite there yet."

As the others continued to offer advice and support, Rosie felt her phone vibrate in her pocket. Slipping it out, she saw a text from Derek: "Have you thought about what I said? Can we meet?"

Rosie stared at the screen, her emotions a tangled mess. Part of her wanted to ignore the message, to focus solely on Maria's crisis. But another part, a part she wasn't entirely comfortable acknowledging, felt a pull towards the familiar comfort Derek represented.

"Everything okay?" Trisha's voice startled Rosie out of her thoughts.

"Oh, yes," Rosie said quickly, pocketing her phone. "Just a text."

Trisha raised an eyebrow but didn't push. "You know," she said quietly, "it's okay to think about your own situation too. We're here for Maria, but we're here for you as well."

Rosie nodded, grateful for the understanding.

As the group began to disperse, Maria insisting she needed some time alone, Rosie found herself lingering in the kitchen.

"Penny for your thoughts?" Lisa asked, joining her at the sink as they washed up the tea things. Rosie sighed, her hands moving mechanically over the dishes.

"Derek wants to meet," she admitted. "To talk about... reconciliation."

Lisa's hands stilled. "Ah," she said. "And how do you feel about that?"

"I don't know," Rosie confessed. "After everything with Maria and David, it feels... complicated."

"Life usually is," Lisa said wryly. "But Rosie, you can't let Maria's situation dictate your choices. Every relationship is different."

"I know," Rosie nodded. "It's just... I was starting to feel like I knew who I was again, you know? Like I was Rosie, not just Derek's wife or Mary's mother. And now..."

"Now you're afraid of losing that if you go back," Lisa finished for her.

"Exactly."

Lisa was quiet for a moment, contemplating. "You know," she said finally, "meeting with Derek doesn't have to mean going back. It could just be... getting closure. Or redefining your relationship on new terms."

Rosie considered this. "You're right," she said slowly. "I suppose I owe it to myself – and to Derek – to at least hear him out."

"That's the spirit," Lisa smiled. "And remember, whatever you decide, we've got your back."

As they finished the washing up, Rosie felt a sense of resolution settling over her. She pulled out her phone and, before she could second-guess herself, typed out a reply to Derek:

"Okay. Let's meet for lunch tomorrow. At Chez Katerina on the High Street at 1 pm."

The response came almost immediately: "I'll be there. Thank you, Rosie." Rosie let out a breath she hadn't realised she'd been holding. For better or worse, she was facing this head-on. Now, another quick call to make – to Mike. She didn't want to lie to him or shield anything from him. She wanted to tell him that she was meeting up with her ex-husband.

MEETING DEREK

The next morning dawned bright and clear, a stark contrast to the emotional turbulence of the previous day. Rosie stood in front of her wardrobe, facing the difficult question: what does one wear to meet their estranged husband?

After much deliberation, she settled on a simple blue dress that Derek had always liked, paired with a new cardigan – a small symbol of the changes in her life. But as she studied her reflection, she wondered if she was trying too hard to recapture something that had long since passed.

As she was applying the last touches to her makeup, her phone buzzed with a flurry of messages from the Sensational Sixties Squad group chat:

Catherine: "Remember, you're strong and beautiful. Don't let him make you feel otherwise."

Julie: "Channel your inner goddess. You've got this!"

Lisa: "Stay true to yourself. We're here if you need us."

Trisha: "If he tries any funny business, I know people who know people. Just saying."

Emma: "Give him hell, Red!"

Rosie chuckled, shaking her head. She was about to reply when another message popped up, this time from Mike:

"Hope you have a good day. Thinking of you."

Her stomach did a little flip at Mike's words. Simple, sweet, and very understanding given her impending lunch with Derek. Rosie sighed, pocketing her phone.

One crisis at a time.

The walk to the restaurant felt both interminable and far too short. With each step, Rosie's mind raced with potential scenarios. What if Derek had changed? What if he hadn't? What if she had changed too much?

As she approached Chez Katerina, she spotted Derek through the window. He was already seated, nervously adjusting his tie. The sight was so familiar, yet somehow foreign - like looking at an old photograph of a place you once knew well but had almost forgotten.

Taking a deep breath, Rosie pushed open the door. The maître d' looked up, his eyebrow raised in polite inquiry.

"I'm meeting someone," Rosie said, gesturing towards Derek. "My... my husband." The word felt strange on her tongue. Ex-husband? Estranged husband? What were they to each other now?

As she approached the table, Derek stood, a tentative smile on his face. "Rosie," he said, his voice warm. "You look lovely."

"Thank you," Rosie replied, suddenly feeling shy. "You look well too."

An awkward moment passed as they both hesitated, unsure whether to hug, shake hands, or simply sit. Derek pulled out her chair, a gesture so reminiscent of their early dating days that Rosie felt a pang of... was it nostalgia? Or something else?

As they settled into their seats, Derek noticed the changes in Rosie. There was a sparkle in her eye that he hadn't seen in years, a confidence in the way she carried herself. "You look... different," he said, immediately regretting how it sounded. "I mean, you look wonderful. Happy."

Rosie smiled a genuine smile that lit up her face. "I am happy, Derek. I've discovered a lot about myself these past few months."

Derek nodded, feeling a mix of admiration and regret. "I've heard about your new friends. The, uh, Sensational Sixties Squad, is it? Mary told me about them. They sound like good fun."

Rosie laughed, the sound both familiar and somehow new to Derek's ears. "Oh yes, they're quite a group. They've shown me that life doesn't end at sixty. It's only just beginning."

As Rosie launched into a story about their latest adventure, Derek found himself captivated. This was a side of Rosie he'd never seen – or perhaps, he realised with a pang, a side he'd never taken the time to see. He'd been so caught up in his own midlife crisis that he'd missed the amazing woman Rosie had always had the potential to be.

"I'm glad," he said softly when she finished, "that you've found this new life. And I... I hope there might be room in it for me."

Rosie smiled at Derek and took a moment to look at her estranged husband. He had aged, of course - they both had. But there was something else, a vulnerability in his eyes that she wasn't used to seeing.

"So," Rosie began, fiddling with her menu, "how have you been?" Derek nodded, taking a deep breath. "I've been... alright. Working a lot. The world feels empty without..." he trailed off, leaving the "you" unspoken but hanging in the air between them.

Rosie felt a twinge of guilt, quickly followed by a flash of anger. It had been his choice to leave, after all. But before she could dwell on it, the waiter appeared to take their order.

"I'll have the salmon salad," Rosie said, then froze as Derek spoke at the same time: "She'll have the salmon salad, and I'll take the steak frites."

Their eyes met, a moment of shared amusement at their synchronicity quickly giving way to awkwardness.

"Sorry," Derek mumbled. "Old habits, I suppose."

As the waiter retreated, Rosie cast about for a safe topic. "Tell me about work then. No plans to retire?" Derek launched into a story about his latest project, and Rosie found herself relaxing slightly. This was familiar territory - listening to Derek talk about his job, nodding in all the right places. It was almost comforting in its familiarity. But as Derek spoke, Rosie's mind wandered. She thought of her friends, of the laughter and adventures they'd shared over the past few months. She thought of Mike, of the spark she'd felt on their date. And she realised that while sitting here with Derek was comfortable, it didn't make her heart race the way it once had.

"Rosie? Are you listening?" Derek's voice snapped her back to the present.

"Sorry," she said, flushing slightly. "I was just..."

But before she could finish her sentence, a commotion near the entrance caught her attention. To her horror and amusement, she saw Emma bobbing through the crowd, followed closely by Lisa, Julie, and Catherine. "Oh, for heaven's sake," Rosie muttered under her breath.

Derek turned to see what had caught her attention, his eyebrows rising in surprise.

"Well, I'll be! Rosie, darling, what a coincidence!" said Emma, her voice ringing out across the restaurant. Rosie closed her eyes briefly, praying for patience. When she opened them, she plastered on a smile.

"Emma! What a surprise. What brings you all here?"

Emma grinned, unrepentant.

"Oh, you know, just thought we'd come and say 'hello'. Mind if we join you?"

Without waiting for an answer, Emma pulled up a chair, the others following suit with varying degrees of embarrassment. Derek looked bewildered but managed a polite smile.

"Hello, I'm Derek. Rosie's..."

"Husband," Emma finished for him, her tone making the word sound like an accusation. "Yes, we've heard all about you."

Lisa, ever the peacemaker, jumped in. "It's lovely to meet you properly, Derek. We saw you in the park, briefly. Rosie's told us so much."

As the others settled in, ordering drinks and effectively hijacking what was supposed to be an intimate lunch, Rosie found herself torn between mortification and relief. On one hand, she was touched by her friends' obvious concern for her wellbeing. On the other, she was a grown woman, perfectly capable of handling lunch with her estranged husband on her own.

The conversation moved on in fits and starts, with Emma peppering Derek with not-so-subtle questions about his intentions, Lisa trying to steer things towards safer topics, Julie waxing poetic about the restaurant's decor, and Catherine looking like she'd rather be anywhere else.

Through it all, Derek remained remarkably composed, answering questions with grace and even managing to charm Julie with his unexpected knowledge of modern art.

As their food arrived - salmon salad for Rosie, steak frites for Derek, and an assortment of dishes for the interlopers - Rosie found herself studying Derek. There was a time when she could read his every expression, and anticipate his every mood. Now, she realised with a start, he was almost a stranger to her.

"So, Derek," Emma said, spearing a piece of asparagus with more force than necessary, "what exactly are your intentions towards our Rosie?"

"Emma!" Lisa hissed, but Derek held up a hand. "It's alright," he said, his eyes never leaving Rosie's face. "I appreciate your concern for Rosie. The truth is, I made a terrible mistake in leaving. I took for granted the wonderful life we had together, and I'm hoping... well, I'm hoping Rosie might give me a chance to make amends."

A hush fell over the table. Rosie felt her cheeks warm under the intensity of Derek's gaze and the expectant looks from her friends. She didn't know what to say. She sat quietly, looking down at her hands until the welcome buzz of her phone gave her the distraction she craved. This was bound to be her daughter. Rosie pulled it out, her heart skipping a beat as she saw Mike's name on the screen.

"Hi Rosie, Just wanted to say I hope your lunch is going well. No pressure, but if you need an escape plan, just say the word and I'll stage a medical emergency ;)"

Rosie smiled at the message, a fact that didn't go unnoticed by Derek or her friends.

"Everything OK?" Derek asked, a hint of tension in his voice. "All fine," Rosie said quickly, tucking her phone away. But the moment had shifted something in her. The warmth she'd felt at Mike's message, and the easy way he made her smile stood in stark contrast to the awkward, tension-filled lunch she was currently enduring.

As the meal progressed, Rosie realised how torn she was. On one hand, there was Derek - familiar, comfortable, a shared history of three decades. On the other, there was the new life she'd been building, filled with friendship, laughter, and the possibility of new love with Mike.

The conversation around her faded into a dull buzz as Rosie's mind whirled with conflicting emotions. She was vaguely aware of Emma regaling the table with an outrageous story, of Derek laughing politely at all the right moments, of Lisa shooting her concerned glances. It wasn't until Derek placed his hand over hers that Rosie snapped back to the present.

"Rosie," he said softly, "I know this is a lot to take in. And I know I'm asking for more than I deserve. But I want you to know that I'm committed to making this work if you'll have me."

Rosie looked into Derek's eyes, seeing the sincerity there. For a moment, she was transported back in time - to their first date, their wedding day, the birth of Mary. So many happy memories, and so much shared history. But then another image flashed in her mind - herself, surrounded by her new friends, laughing freely in a way she hadn't in years. And Mike's face, kind and understanding, offering her a future unburdened by past mistakes.

"I... I need some time to think, Derek," Rosie said finally. "This isn't a decision I can make lightly."

Derek nodded, disappointment clear in his eyes but also a glimmer of hope. "I understand. And I'll wait, Rosie. For as long as it takes."

As the lunch drew to a close, Rosie felt emotionally drained. Her friends, seeming to sense her need for space, made their excuses and left, but not before Emma could whisper in her ear, "Remember, you're the prize here, not him."

Derek walked Rosie to the door of the restaurant, an echo of countless dates from their past. "Thank you for meeting me," he said softly. "And for... for being open to the possibility."

Rosie managed a small smile. "Thank you for being

honest about your feelings. I... I'll be in touch, Derek. I promise."

They parted with an awkward half-hug. As she walked home, Rosie realised she was at a crossroads. To the left lay the path to her old life with Derek, familiar and comfortable. To the right, the route to her new life, where possibility and uncertainty waited. For a moment, Rosie hesitated. Then, almost of their own accord, her feet turned right. She wasn't ready to make any big decisions yet, but she knew one thing for certain - whatever choice she made, it would be on her terms.

As she walked, her phone buzzed again. This time, it was a message from the Sensational Sixties Squad group chat: Emma: "Well, that was certainly interesting. You okay, Red?"

Lisa: "We're here if you need to talk, Rosie."

Julie: "I thought Derek seemed nice. But it's your decision, of course."

Catherine: "Just remember, you deserve to be happy. Whatever that looks like for you."

Rosie smiled. She was about to reply when another message came through, this time from Mike: "No medical emergencies required, I hope? If you're free later, I'd love to hear about your day. No pressure, of course."

Without overthinking it, she typed out a reply: "Actually, a chat would be lovely. Meet you at the park in an hour?"

Mike's response arrived almost immediately: "I'll be there. Looking forward to it."

As Rosie continued her walk home, she felt a curious mix of emotions. The lunch with Derek had stirred up old memories and emotions, but it had also clarified something for Rosie. She wasn't the same woman she had been when Derek left. She had grown, changed, and discovered new parts of herself. And while part of her would always care for

Derek, she wasn't sure if there was room in her new life for old patterns.

As she approached her house, Rosie made a decision. She would take things one day at a time. She would be honest with both Derek and Mike about her feelings and her uncertainties. And most importantly, she would prioritise her own happiness and growth.

HOUSE OF CHAOS

Rosie stood in her kitchen, surveying the chaos that had overtaken her once-peaceful home. Dishes were piled high in the sink, mismatched shoes littered the floor, and the dining table had disappeared under a mountain of magazines, makeup, and what appeared to be half of Mary's wardrobe.

Her daughter had only come round to collect Elvis but seemed to have brought most of the contents of her house with her. Upstairs she could hear Maria pottering around, tidying up.

"How on earth did I end up running a halfway house for the displaced?" she muttered to herself, reaching for the kettle.

If ever there was a time for a strong cup of tea, this was it.

Just as the kettle began to whistle, a crash from upstairs made Rosie wince.

"Everything's fine!" a voice called out, not quite masking the note of panic. "Just a small...accident!"

"Be careful, Mary," bellowed Rosie.

"I'm here, don't worry," shouted Maria.

Rosie closed her eyes, counted to ten, and poured her tea. It had been three days since Maria had shown up on her doorstep, suitcase in hand, mascara streaking her cheeks.

"Maria? Goodness, what's happened?" Rosie had asked, alarmed by her friend's red-rimmed eyes and trembling chin.

Maria opened her mouth to speak, but all that came out was a choked sob. Without a word, Rosie pulled her into a tight embrace, ushering her inside and kicking the door shut behind them.

"There, there," Rosie soothed, patting Maria's back as she continued to shake with silent sobs. "Let's get you settled, and then you can tell me all about it. How does a nice cuppa sound?"

Maria nodded weakly against Rosie's shoulder, allowing herself to be led into the cosy living room. Rosie deposited her gently on the sofa, tucking a soft throw around her shoulders before bustling off to the kitchen to put the kettle on. When she returned a few minutes later, armed with a tray of tea and biscuits, Maria had managed to compose herself somewhat. Her eyes were still puffy, and her usually immaculate hair was a mess, but she'd stopped crying at least.

"Now then," Rosie said gently, pressing a warm mug into Maria's hands. "What's all this about? Has something happened with David?"

At the mention of her husband's name, Maria's face crumpled again. "Oh, Rosie," she whispered, her voice raw with pain. "He's... he's been having an affair."

Rosie felt her heart drop. "Oh, Maria. I'm so sorry. Are you certain?"

Maria nodded miserably. "You know when we saw them together in the park? David and this... this girl. She can't be more than thirty-five. At first, I thought there must be some explanation. Perhaps she was a colleague or a friend's daughter. But the way he was looking at her..." She trailed off, fresh tears spilling down her cheeks.

Rosie reached out and squeezed Maria's hand. "What happened then? Did you confront him?"

"I couldn't bear to," Maria admitted. "I went home and waited for him, pretending everything was normal. But he must have sensed something was off because he kept asking if I was alright. And then... and then he just blurted it out."

She took a shaky breath, staring down into her tea as if it held the answers to the universe. "He said he was sorry, that he never meant for it to happen. And then he told me... oh, Rosie, it wasn't just this one. There have been others."

Rosie felt a flare of anger towards David. How dare he hurt Maria like this? Sweet, kind Maria who colour-coded her spice rack and always remembered everyone's birthdays.

"Oh, my dear," Rosie murmured, pulling Maria into another hug. "I can't imagine how you must be feeling."

Maria clung to her, her words muffled against Rosie's shoulder. "I don't know how to go on, Rosie. I love him so much. We've been together for thirty years. How could he throw all that away?"

As Maria's sobs subsided, she pulled back, wiping her eyes with a tissue. "You should have been there at our twenty-fifth-anniversary party," she said, a wistful smile flickering across her face. "He surprised me with a second honeymoon. Two weeks in Italy, just like when we were first married. It was magical, Rosie. We walked hand in hand through the streets of Rome, ate gelato by the Trevi Fountain, danced under the stars in Venice..."

Her voice cracked. "How could he do this to us? It was all a lie. It was a horrible, mean lie."

"Perhaps it wasn't all a lie," Rosie said gently. "The good

times you shared, the love you felt – that was real, Maria. David's actions now don't negate all those years of happiness."

Maria shook her head, her expression hardening. "But how can I trust any of it now? How do I know he wasn't thinking of someone else every time he told me he loved me?"

Rosie sighed, wishing she had the right words to ease her friend's pain. "I don't have all the answers. But I do know that you're stronger than you think. You'll get through this, one day at a time. And you won't have to do it alone."

Maria looked up, her eyes wide and vulnerable. "What do you mean?"

"Well," Rosie said, straightening up with determination, "for starters, you're staying here tonight. No arguments. I won't have you going back to that house, not when the wounds are so fresh."

"Oh, Rosie, I couldn't possibly impose—"

"Nonsense," Rosie cut her off firmly. "What are friends for if not for providing a shoulder to cry on and a spare room in times of crisis? Besides, we can stay up late, eat too much ice cream, and plot our revenge on all the men who've ever wronged us."

That startled a watery chuckle out of Maria. "I'm not sure I'm up for revenge plotting just yet."

"Fair enough," Rosie conceded. "How about we start with some mindless telly and a large glass of wine instead? I think I've got a bottle of that Rioja you like squirrelled away somewhere."

As Rosie bustled about, fetching wine and fluffing pillows, she kept a watchful eye on Maria. Her friend still looked shell-shocked and devastated, but there was a tiny spark of something in her eyes now. Determination, perhaps. Or the first flickering of hope. Later that evening, as they sat side by side on the sofa, wine glasses in hand and some ridiculous reality show playing in the background, Maria turned to Rosie.

"Thank you," she said softly. "I don't know what I'd do without you. Without all of you," she added, no doubt thinking of Emma, Lisa, and the others. Rosie smiled, reaching out to squeeze Maria's hand.

"That's what the Sensational Sixties Squad is for, love. We've weathered our fair share of storms, you and I. We'll weather this one too."

Maria nodded, a ghost of a smile touching her lips. "I suppose we will. Though I'm not feeling particularly sensational at the moment."

"Give it time," Rosie assured her. "Before you know it, you'll be out there painting the town red with the rest of us. But for now, it's okay to not be okay. You take all the time you need to grieve and heal. We'll be right here beside you every step of the way."

As Maria leaned her head on Rosie's shoulder, both women fell silent, lost in thought. Rosie's mind wandered to her own failed marriage, to the pain and betrayal she'd felt when Derek left. She'd never imagined she'd find happiness again, let alone the kind of deep, abiding friendship she now shared.

Life had a funny way of surprising you. Just when you thought it was all over, that there were no more adventures to be had, it threw you a curveball. Sometimes those curveballs hurt like hell, but they could also lead you to unexpected joys.

She glanced down at Maria, who had dozed off, her face finally peaceful in sleep. With a contented sigh, Rosie settled back into the sofa, letting the gentle drone of the television wash over her. Tomorrow would bring its own trials, but for now, this was enough – this quiet moment of friendship, of shared pain and shared strength.

In the morning, they would rally the troops, and plan their next move. But tonight, they would simply be two friends, supporting each other through the storms of life, one cup of tea and one glass of wine at a time.

SPA DAY

Maria had had good days and bad days since the night she'd turned up, unannounced on Rosie's doorstep.

Some nights Rosie would hear her crying in her room, other days, Maria would be up and about, planning a bright and wonderful life without David.

Having Maria stay had been fun. It helped that the woman was spotlessly clean and organised. Rosie had never seen anything like it. No sooner had she lain a teaspoon in a saucer that Maria had picked it up and washed it.

Mary was a different character altogether. She was a thundering ball of chaos, flying through the house, knocking things over and bashing into every piece of furniture she passed. As Rosie got up to move some of Mary's clothes off the table, the doorbell rang, and a disconsolate Catherine stood on the doorstep.

"Richard's at it again," Catherine said without preamble, her voice tight with frustration. "He showed up at my book club meeting and told everyone I was 'too fragile' to be out on my own. Can you believe it? We've been divorced for five years, and he still thinks he can control my life!"

"Oh, angel. Come in. I'll put the kettle on."

Catherine settled at the kitchen table, dumping an enormous handbag that seemed to contain half her possessions. Rosie smiled to herself. How had her orderly life spiralled into this sitcom-worthy scenario? Not that she objected. There was something anarchic about it all and, surprisingly, that appealed to her.

She texted Emma to let her know that the troops were amassing at hers, and if Emma fancied coming over, she was very welcome.

"Is that you, Catherine?" Maria shouted from upstairs, before appearing at the door in a headscarf that made her look like a 1940s housewife. "Oh good, I need your opinion. Do you think I should dye my hair red? David always hated red hair, and said it was too 'attention-seeking'."

Catherine blinked, momentarily stunned by Maria's suggestion. She couldn't think of anyone in the world less likely to dye her hair red.

"Um, well, I suppose if it would make you happy..."

"Wonderful. I'll just pop to the shops and get some dye. I need to pick up some cleaning products and some paint for the windowsill. Rosie, you don't mind if I borrow your car, do you? Mine's still at the house, and I can't bear to go back there just yet."

Before Rosie could formulate a response, Maria had taken the car keys and was out the door, hair scarf and all.

"Well," Rosie said faintly, "I suppose that's one way to make a statement at the supermarket."

Catherine giggled, a sound so unexpected that Rosie couldn't help but join in. Soon, they were both howling with laughter, the absurdity of the situation finally hitting home.

"Oh dear," Catherine gasped, wiping tears from her eyes.

"What a pair we are. Two divorced women becoming hysterical over a woman sporting a hair scarf."

"But she did look exactly like that woman from the poster – the one encouraging women to get involved in the war effort. Do you remember that? The woman had a red, spotty headscarf on and was flexing her biceps."

"No, I don't remember it from the war but then you're considerably older than me."

"Oy, stop that right there. I don't remember the poster from the 40s. I remember seeing it in history books."

"Yeah right," said Catherine with a smile. She giggled to herself and turned to Rosie. "This is such fun, isn't it? A group of women hanging out together. It's like being a teenager again."

"Speak for yourself," Rosie chuckled. "I never had this much excitement as a teenager."

Their chat was interrupted by the sound of a key in the lock, heralding the arrival of Emma who burst through the door, laden with shopping bags. "I've brought reinforcements. Wine, chocolate, and so many crisps that we could paper the walls in them. By the way, your key was in the door."

"Oh," said Rosie, taking it from Emma. "There are so many people with my keys at the moment, this could be anyone's."

Emma began unpacking her bags, revealing an alarming array of junk food and beauty products. "We're having a girls' day," she said, as if every meeting of the Sensational Sixties squad was anything but a 'girls' day.'

"We all need cheering up. Now, where do you keep your wine glasses?"

Before Rosie could answer, the front door burst open again, this time revealing Maria, her arms full of shopping bags, her hair still wrapped in a hair scarf."

"I'm back!" she called out. "And I've got... oh! Hello, Emma, when did you get here? Oh, never mind, you're just in time. I've got hair dye, a new wardrobe, and... is that wine I see? Perfect!"

"Yes, there's plenty of wine. Where have you been? Out helping the war effort? Working in a munitions factory or something?"

Maria took the scarf out of her hair. "What is wrong with you all?" she asked. "I like to keep my hair clean and tidy. I always wear this at home. I didn't realise it would become such a conversation starter."

"Starting conversations is all good. Anyway, you don't have to worry about what you look like, because we are going to transform our appearances while drinking wine and gossiping."

As Emma unloaded enough beauty products to open a small branch of Boots, the others looked on. "Why on earth do we need all this?" asked Catherine. "And where has it come from? You've never struck me as a beauty products kind of woman."

"Me? No. I never use any of it, but the woman who lives next door is a beauty PR, and she is given lots of freebies. She brought a big bag full round, so I've brought the bag here"

"Well, that's very generous of her. Let 'Operation Makeover' begin," said Rosie, looking through the vast array of products. There were creams, lotions and potions for every possible problem in every area of the body.

Green cream to combat redness, conditioning oil for eyelashes, neck creams, hair oil, facial massaging contraptions…it was ridiculous. Who had time to do all this?

"No, I don't know what it's all for either," said Emma, reading Rosie's mind. "There are products here to cure beauty issues that I didn't know existed."

While Emma and Rosie looked askance at the array of products, Catherine dived in.

"Oooo...tweezers," she said. "I've always wanted to get my eyebrows done."

Rosie didn't feel quite so adrift at this point. At least she was aware of the value of tweezers and regularly had her eyebrows tended to.

"Come on then," said Emma, lifting the tweezers like a weapon and moving in the direction of Catherine's face. "Let's sort out these big, fat caterpillars for you."

Rosie found herself swept along on the tide of giggling, gossiping, and general mayhem. She had her toenails painted by Catherine, had covered herself in a face masque that had made her skin tingle and had rubbed 'elbow defender' into her rough elbows.

As evening fell, they ordered in an alarming amount of Chinese food and settled in the living room, surrounded by the detritus of their 'spa day.'

"You know," Maria said, admiring her newly red locks in a hand mirror, "I haven't had this much fun in years. David always said these kinds of girls' nights were frivolous."

"Well, David's an idiot," Emma declared, raising her wine glass in a toast. "Here's to frivolity, and to friends who don't judge you for it!"

As they clinked glasses, a loud banging on the front door made them all jump.

"Rosie!" a man's voice called out. "I know Catherine's in there. Tell her to come out at once!"

Catherine paled, shrinking back into the sofa. "It's Richard," she whispered. "How did he find me?"

Rosie felt a surge of protective anger. She marched to the door and flung it open, coming face to face with a red-faced Richard.

"Can I help you?" she asked coldly. Richard tried to peer around her.

"Where's Catherine? I know she's here. She needs to come home now. She's not well, she shouldn't be out on her own."

"I can assure you," Rosie said, drawing herself up to her full height, "that Catherine is perfectly fine. She's a grown woman, fully capable of making her own decisions. And right now, she's decided to stay here with her friends."

"How dare you talk to me like that," Richard began, but he was cut off by Emma, who had appeared at Rosie's shoulder.

"We'll talk to you in any way we choose. You have no right to tell Catherine what she can and can't do. You have no right to follow her and make demands. This is plain harassment. Either go away and leave her alone, or I'll call the police."

Richard sputtered, clearly unused to being spoken to in such a manner.

"This isn't over," he growled, but he turned and stomped back to his car.

"No, it's not," Emma growled back. "Because if you ever come here again we'll ring the police. You have been warned."

As Rosie closed the door, she turned to find Catherine staring at her with wide eyes.

"Thank you," Catherine whispered. "Both of you. I've never... I mean, I didn't know how to..."

"Oh, come here, you silly goose," Emma said, pulling Catherine into a hug. "That's what friends are for. Now, who wants more wine?"

As they settled back in the living room, Rosie marvelled at the turn her life had taken. A month ago, she would have been horrified at the mess, the noise, the sheer chaos of it all. But now...

"You know," she said, surprising herself, "I have a spare

room or two upstairs. If either of you needs a place to stay for a while, they're yours."

Maria and Catherine exchanged glances, then looked back at Rosie with identical expressions of gratitude and relief.

"Are you sure?" Maria asked. "We don't want to impose..."

Rosie waved away their concerns. "Impose away. To tell you the truth, I'm rather enjoying the company."

As the evening wore on, filled with more laughter, more wine, and increasingly outrageous plans for their 'new lives,' Rosie felt a warmth that had nothing to do with the alcohol. This, she realised, was what she'd been missing all these years. Not just companionship, but true friendship. The kind where you could show up on someone's doorstep in crisis and be met with open arms and a willing ear.

It was well past midnight when they finally began to settle down for the night. Rosie provided Catherine with pyjamas, while Maria insisted on sleeping in a slinky nightgown she'd bought on her shopping spree ("David always said nightgowns were for grannies. Well, I'll show him!").

As Rosie lay in bed, listening to the unfamiliar sounds of other people moving about her house, she couldn't keep the smile off her face. Yes, her life had become chaotic. Yes, her house was a mess. And yes, she now apparently had two new roommates. But the first time in longer than she cared to admit, Rosie felt truly alive. She was just drifting off to sleep when a crash from downstairs jolted her awake.

"Sorry!" Catherine's voice called out. "Just getting a glass of water. Um, Rosie? Where do you keep the dustpan?"

"I've got it in my room," shouted Maria. "Sorry. You know what I'm like, I have a genetic need to clean all the time."

Rosie chuckled, shaking her head. Life with her new housemates was certainly going to be interesting.

The next morning dawned bright and early, much to the chagrin of three slightly hungover women.

Rosie, always the early riser, found herself tiptoeing around her own kitchen, trying not to wake her guests. Her efforts were in vain, however, as Maria stumbled down the stairs, her new red hair shining in the early morning sunshine, still wearing the slinky nightgown from the night before.

"Coffee," she groaned, slumping into a kitchen chair. "I need coffee. And possibly a new head."

Rosie chuckled, sliding a steaming mug across the table. "Here you go. How are you feeling this morning? Any regrets about the hair?"

Maria patted her head gingerly, then smiled. "You know what? Not a single one. David can take his opinions and shove them where the sun doesn't shine."

"That's the spirit," Catherine said, appearing in the doorway. She looked surprisingly chipper for someone who had consumed her body weight in wine the night before.

"Are you all OK to get your own breakfasts? Just help yourself to anything. I'm meeting Mary for a quick catch-up. I'll be back in about an hour.

"No problem – you go and see Mary and say 'hi' from us."

THE CAFÉ BUZZED with the quiet chatter of patrons and the hiss of the espresso machine. Rosie sat across from Mary, watching her daughter encouraging the twins to eat, while simultaneously trying to eat a scone.

"Here, let me help," Rosie offered, kissing the children on their heads and persuading them to eat their sandwiches.

She caught Mary studying her with an odd expression.

"What is it? Do I have jam on my face?"

Mary shook her head, a smile tugging at her lips. "No, it's not that. It's just... you seem different, Mum. Happier."

Rosie felt a warmth spread through her chest. "Do I?"

"You're practically glowing," Mary confirmed. "I haven't seen you like this in years. Is it the new friends? Or perhaps this mysterious Mike I've been hearing about?"

Rosie felt a blush creep up her cheeks. "It's everything, I suppose. The friends, Mike, the adventures we've been having. I feel like I'm finally living, Mary, not just existing."

Mary reached across and squeezed her mother's hand. "I'm so glad, Mum. You deserve this happiness. And for what it's worth, I think Dad sees it too. He mentioned how different you seemed when he saw you last."

Rosie's smile faltered slightly. "Your father... well, that's complicated. But let's not dwell on that. Tell me more about what the twins have been up to."

As Mary launched into a story about the children's latest antics, Rosie felt a surge of gratitude. Not just for her new lease on life, but for this moment of connection with her daughter.

By the time Rosie arrived back home, she'd made some important decisions.

"Ladies," she said, bursting through the door. "We need a house meeting." Catherine and Maria walked into the kitchen and sat at the big dining room table. "I just wanted to say that you are both welcome to stay as long as you need. As long as you want. I'm enjoying your company. There's no pressure on either of you to leave. I just wanted you both to know that. I'm rather enjoying having my very own sitcom playing out in my living room."

"Oh, thank you," they both said, hugging Rosie. "You are so kind to put up with us. Thank you."

"No, you are very welcome."

As they cleared away the breakfast dishes, chattering

about their plans for the day (Maria was determined to revamp her entire wardrobe, while Catherine wanted to start a blog about life after divorce), the doorbell rang, interrupting their planning session. Rosie opened it to find Emma, Lisa, Julie, and Trisha on her doorstep, all looking far too perky for this time of the morning.

"Hello, sunshine!" Emma called out. "We've come to check on our refugees. How's life in Casa del Chaos?"

Rosie ushered them in, explaining the events of the previous night.

"Well," Lisa said, once Rosie had finished her tale, "it seems like you've had quite the adventure. Are you sure you're okay with all this, Rosie? It's a big change from your usual routine."

Rosie looked around at the women gathered in her kitchen - Maria with her flame-red hair, Catherine with her newfound confidence, Emma with her irrepressible spirit... She thought about the laughter that now filled her home, the late-night chats, and the sense of purpose she felt in helping her friends through their own crises.

"You know what?" she said, a slow smile spreading across her face. "I've never been better. It turns out, a little chaos is just what I needed."

THE SUPERMARKET INCIDENT

Rosie stood in her kitchen, frowning at the depleted contents of her refrigerator. With three women now living under her roof, food seemed to vanish at an alarming rate. She sighed, closed the door and turned to face her housemates.

"Right," she announced, "we need to go shopping. This house has more women than food, and that's a situation I never thought I'd find myself in."

Maria looked up from her fashion magazine, her newly dyed red hair catching the sunlight. "Ooh, shopping! I love shopping. Though I suppose you mean the boring kind with vegetables, not the fun kind with shoes."

Catherine, who had been furiously typing away at her new blog, 'Life Begins at Divorce,' barely glanced up. "Do we have to? I'm right in the middle of a scathing post about Richard's controlling behaviour. Did you know he once tried to dictate what colour I painted my toenails?"

Rosie raised an eyebrow. "Unless you're planning to eat your laptop, yes, we have to. Come on, it'll be fun. We'll make an outing of it."

BERNICE BLOOM

As Catherine finished writing and put away her computer, the doorbell rang. Emma's voice carried through the letterbox, "Oi, you lot! We've come to rescue you from suburban boredom!"

Rosie opened the door to find Emma, Lisa, Julie, and Trisha on her doorstep, all looking far too excited for a random Tuesday morning. "Perfect timing," Rosie said, ushering them in. "We were just about to go grocery shopping. Want to join us?"

Emma's face fell. "Grocery shopping? Boring! I was thinking more along the lines of sky diving or perhaps a nice protest march."

Lisa rolled her eyes. "Don't be dramatic, Emma. Grocery shopping can be fun with the right company. Besides," she added with a mischievous glint in her eye, "I heard the new Waitrose has a wine-tasting section."

Seven pairs of eyes lit up simultaneously.

"Well," Trisha said, a slow smile spreading across her face, "we wouldn't want to miss out on expanding our palates, would we?"

And so, twenty minutes later, the Sensational Sixties Squad found themselves entering the sliding doors of Waitrose, armed with shopping lists and a joy usually reserved for taking a bra off at the end of the day.

"Right," Rosie said, trying to instil some order, "let's start with the essentials. Fruits, vegetables, bread..."

"Wine tasting!" Emma interrupted, already making a beeline for the back of the store.

"Emma!" Rosie called after her, but it was too late. The others had caught the scent of adventure (and alcohol) and were following in Emma's wake like a line of ducklings.

Rosie sighed, grabbed a shopping trolley, and followed. By the time she caught up, Emma was already chatting up the young man running the wine-tasting booth.

"Now, darling," Emma was saying, fluttering her eyelashes in a way that was more alarming than alluring, "let's see what you've got, shall we?"

The poor lad, who looked barely out of his teens, gulped nervously.

"I, um, I suppose so. We do have a lovely Chardonnay that's just been opened..."

As he poured generous 'samples' into their tasting glasses, Rosie felt a moment of misgiving.

"Perhaps we should finish the shopping first," she suggested weakly. But her protest was drowned out by the clink of glasses and Emma's enthusiastic,

"Cheers, ladies! Here's to grocery shopping with style!"

One sample turned into two, then three. Thank goodness the shop was close enough to Rosie's house that they had been able to walk there. The young man in charge of the wine-tasting booth, initially flustered, soon found himself enjoying the attention of seven vivacious women who laughed at his jokes and seemed genuinely interested in his explanation of wine regions.

"You know," Maria said, her cheeks flushed pink from more than just the previous evening's makeover, "David never let me drink wine. He said it made me silly."

"Silly is good," Julie declared, raising her glass in a toast. "Here's to being silly, and to hell with men who don't appreciate it!"

They all cheered, drawing curious glances from nearby shoppers. Rosie, who had been nursing her first glass, realised with a start that they had been at the shop for nearly half an hour and hadn't bought a single grocery item.

"Come on, ladies," she said, trying to herd them towards the produce section. "Let's at least pretend we came here to shop."

Giggling like schoolgirls, they followed Rosie, weaving slightly as they navigated the aisles.

Catherine insisted on stopping at every free sample stand they passed, accumulating an impressive collection of tiny cups and toothpicks in her handbag.

"Ooh, look!" Emma exclaimed, holding up a pineapple. "Doesn't this remind you of Richard's hair when he turned up at the house last night?"

The image of Catherine's usually impeccably groomed husband with a pineapple-shaped bedhead sent them into fits of laughter. As they moved through the store, their volume seemed to increase in direct proportion to the amount of wine they had consumed.

Rosie found herself shushing them repeatedly, to little effect.

"So, Rosie," Emma said loudly as they perused the cereal aisle, "have you decided between Derek and Mike yet? Because personally, I think you should go for Mike. He's got that silver fox thing going on."

Rosie felt her face flame as several heads turned in their direction. "Emma!" she said with a smile. "Could we perhaps not discuss my love life in the middle of Waitrose?"

But Emma was on a roll. "I'm just saying, darling, you deserve someone who appreciates you. Someone who won't run off with his midlife crisis on legs."

"Yes!" Maria chimed in, waving a box of Weetabix for emphasis. "Men are like cereals. You think you want the sugary, exciting one, but in the end, you're better off with the reliable bran that keeps you regular!"

This profound statement was met with raucous laughter and a round of applause that echoed through the store.

"Ladies, please," Rosie pleaded, torn between mortification and the urge to laugh along with them. "Let's try to keep it down, shall we?"

This was a shop she frequented regularly, as did Derek, and she imagined Mike did too. They all lived so near to one another. Perhaps she was being paranoid, but she felt it was one thing laughing and joking about this in private but she didn't want to be overheard laughing about it in public.

"Are you OK?" asked Emma. "Have I upset you?"

"No. I just feel awkward chatting about it all in public. Everyone I know uses this supermarket, I don't want to be heard mocking Derek or anything. He's Mary's father. I just feel awkward about it."

There was something else as well. While the others all felt she should throw herself into Mike's arms, she felt huge warmth towards Derek. She was torn. She wanted time to think about it all in private and not debate it in the middle of a crowded supermarket.

"Sure," said Emma. "You're right. I won't mention it again."

As they moved round to the freezer section, Catherine leaned over and looked at the frozen vegetables. "You know. I haven't had sex in so long, I think my lady bits might have frozen over. Just like those cauliflower florets."

Julie nearly choked on the cheese sample she'd been munching. "Catherine!" she gasped, equal parts scandalized and amused. "I never knew you had it in you!"

"That's the problem," Catherine replied mournfully. "Nothing's been in me for years."

This set them off again, their laughter bouncing off the freezer doors and causing a group of teenagers to stare at them in a mixture of horror and fascination.

Rosie, who had been attempting to shop amidst the chaos, realised they had attracted the attention of a stern-looking man in a manager's uniform. He was striding towards them with purpose, his face set in a disapproving frown.

"Oh dear," Rosie murmured. "Ladies, I think we might be in trouble."

But the others were oblivious, now engaged in a heated debate about the merits of various personal lubricants they had spotted in the health and beauty aisle.

"Excuse me, ladies," the manager said as he reached them, his voice clipped. "I'm going to have to ask you to lower your voices. We've had complaints from other customers about the... nature of your conversation."

Emma, never one to back down from authority, drew herself up to her full height (which, admittedly, was quite imposing). "Now see here, young man," she began, jabbing a finger at his chest. "We are paying customers, and we have every right to discuss whatever we please. Just because some prudes can't handle a bit of frank discussion about sexual health-"

"Emma!" Lisa interjected, trying to salvage the situation. "I'm so sorry, sir. We'll keep it down, won't we, ladies?"

There was a mumbled chorus of agreement, though Rosie noticed Emma rolling her eyes dramatically. The manager nodded stiffly.

"I'd be grateful if you would. This is a family shop. We have to be mindful of all our customers."

As he walked away, Emma muttered, "Family shop, my arse. Where do they think families come from? The stork?"

This set them off again, their laughter only slightly muffled by their attempts to contain it. Rosie, sensing disaster on the horizon, tried to steer them towards the checkouts.

"Come on, let's pay for these and head home. I think we've had quite enough excitement for one day."

But fate, it seemed, had other plans. As they rounded the corner into the toiletries aisle, they came face to face with David, Maria's estranged husband, accompanied by a young woman who was most definitely not his colleague. She looked suspiciously like the woman they had seen him in the park with. The silence that fell was deafening. Maria, her eyes wide with shock, stood frozen, a pack of toilet paper clutched to her chest like a shield.

David looked like he'd seen a ghost - or rather, seven very tipsy ghosts, all staring at him accusingly. It was Emma who broke the silence.

"Well, well, well," she said."If it isn't the man of the hour. Tell me, David, does your little friend here know you're married?"

The young woman looked bewildered, her eyes darting between David and the group of women who were now forming a protective circle around Maria.

David, to his credit, looked thoroughly ashamed. "Maria," he began, "I can explain."

But Maria, fuelled by wine and righteous anger and flanked by her friends, found her voice. "Explain? EXPLAIN? You explained before. That's why I moved out. You are a lying, cheating, manipulative excuse for a man. I don't want any more explanations. I want a divorce."

"A divorce? Don't be ridiculous."

The attractive young woman looked up. "You are married? You told me you were divorced."

"Shhh…" said David, aggressively. "This has nothing to do with you."

"Really? Nothing to do with me? Fine. In that case, I'm off."

"No, don't go. For God's sake. What's wrong with women? Why are you all such drama queens?"

Maria had heard enough. Before her husband had realised what was happening, she had hurled the pack of toilet paper at his head. Her aim, unfortunately, was less than perfect, so the pack sailed past David and knocked over a carefully constructed display of shampoo bottles, sending them clattering to the floor in a tsunami of hair care products.

The crash echoed through the store, followed by a moment of stunned silence. Then, chaos erupted. Emma, seizing the moment, grabbed another pack of toilet paper and lobbed it at David, this time hitting her mark.

"That's for every time you made Maria feel less than the amazing woman she is!" she yelled.

Seeing their friend in distress, the other women joined in. Soon, the air was filled with flying toilet paper, cotton balls, and the occasional bottle of shampoo. David beat a hasty retreat, ducking and weaving to avoid the barrage of toiletries while swearing at the women and telling them how childish they were.

As soon as he was out of sight, a cheer went up from the Sensational Sixties Squad. Their victory was short-lived, however. The manager, alerted by the commotion, came running down the aisle. When he saw who was causing all the trouble, his face went purple with rage.

"That's it!" he bellowed. "Out! All of you, out of my store this instant!"

Rosie, mortified, tried to apologise. "We're so sorry, we'll clean this up…" she started.

But the manager was having none of it. "Out!" he repeated, pointing towards the exit.

Gathering what little dignity they had left, the women made their way to the front of the store, past gawking customers and whispering employees. As they stepped out into the parking lot, the reality of what had just transpired began to sink in. For a moment, they all stood in silence, looking at each other with a mixture of shock and barely suppressed mirth.

"Well, I'm glad we managed to conduct a basic shopping

trip without bringing huge embarrassment upon ourselves," said Rosie.

Then, as if on cue, they all burst into laughter.

"Did you see David's face?" Maria gasped, wiping tears from her eyes. "I don't think I've ever seen him move so fast!"

"Forget David," Trisha chortled. "Did you see the manager? I thought he was going to explode!"

"Well, ladies," said Rosie, unable to keep the smile from her face, "I think we can safely say that was the most eventful grocery trip in history."

"Hear, hear!" Emma cheered. "Now, who's for a takeaway? I don't know about you lot, but all that excitement has made me peckish."

"You know, I've just realised something important," said Maria. "Life after sixty isn't about slowing down or fading away. It's about seizing every moment and laughing in the face of adversity. We might only have 20 years left…we haven't got time for excusing bad behaviour and meekly backing away when there's trouble."

* * *

THE PUB WAS DIMLY LIT, the air thick with smoke and the murmur of conversation. Richard sat at a corner table, surrounded by his old army mates. Empty pint glasses littered the table, a testament to the hours they'd spent reminiscing about their glory days.

"I'm telling you, lads," Richard slurred, his fist coming down hard on the table, "civvy life's a bloody nightmare. No order, no discipline. And the women? They've got no respect for authority."

His mate, Tom, clapped him on the shoulder. "Still having trouble with the missus, eh?"

Richard's face darkened. "Ex-missus. Catherine's got it in

her head that she can manage without me. Ha! She wouldn't last a day in the real world without my guidance. She's got all these 'friends' – a bunch of dopey old women. She spends all her time with them and they're trying to keep me away from her."

"Maybe it's time to let her go, mate," another friend, Steve, suggested gently. "Find yourself a nice young bird, start fresh."

Richard's eyes flashed dangerously. "Let her go? Not bloody likely. Catherine's my wife, and I'll be damned if I let a bunch of meddling old biddies turn her against me. No, I've got a plan. I'll show her she needs me. One way or another, I'll get her back where she belongs."

As his mates exchanged worried glances, Richard drained his pint, his mind already plotting his next move. He'd spent his life giving orders and having them obeyed. He wasn't about to let Catherine defy him now.

RICHARD'S REVENGE

~~~~

*R*osie peered out from behind her living room curtains, her eyes narrowed as she scanned the quiet suburban street. To the casual observer, it was a perfectly ordinary Friday afternoon. But Rosie knew better. Somewhere out there, lurking behind a hedge or possibly disguised as a particularly lumpy mailbox, was Richard.

"Any sign of him?" Catherine's anxious voice came from behind her.

Rosie shook her head, letting the curtain fall back into place. "Not yet. But he's out there, Catherine. I can feel it in my bunions."

It had been three days since Richard had started his one-man crusade to "protect" Catherine from the supposedly nefarious influence of her new friends.

What had begun as the occasional drive-by had escalated into full-blown stalking, with Richard popping up at all hours like a particularly persistent whack-a-mole.

"I still can't believe he followed me to my dental appointment," Catherine moaned, collapsing onto the sofa. "Who does that? I mean, what did he think I was going to do? Run off with the hygienist?"

Maria, who had been stress-baking in the kitchen (resulting in enough muffins to feed a small army), poked her head around the door. "Maybe he thought you were getting your teeth whitened to impress a new man," she suggested, brandishing a flour-covered spatula. "You know how Richard is about your appearance."

Catherine rolled her eyes. "Yes, because nothing says 'hot date' like 'open wide and say ah.'"

The doorbell rang, making them all jump. Rosie approached it cautiously, half-expecting to find Richard on the other side with a bouquet and a court order. Instead, she opened the door to find Emma, Lisa, Julie, and Trisha, all looking suspiciously cheerful.

"Hello, darlings!" Emma trilled, sweeping past Rosie with the air of someone about to announce a particularly thrilling adventure. "We've come to join Operation: Ditch the Dick!"

Rosie blinked. "Operation what now?"

Lisa, ever the voice of reason, explained as they all filed into the living room. "We've decided that we can't let Richard terrorise Catherine like this. And it can't be up to you guys to sort it out alone. We're all in this together, so we've come to offer backup."

So, we're going to set up a neighbourhood watch. Of sorts."

"Of sorts?" Rosie echoed, a sense of foreboding creeping over her.

"Well," Julie chimed in, her artistic enthusiasm evident, "we thought we could take turns keeping an eye out for Richard. But to avoid suspicion, we'll need disguises!"

With a flourish, she produced a large bag that seemed to contain every rejected costume from the local amateur dramatic society. Catherine's eyes widened in alarm.

"Disguises? Oh, I don't know about this..."

But Emma was already elbow-deep in the bag, pulling out a series of increasingly ridiculous outfits.

"Nonsense, darling. It'll be fun! Look, I've got dibs on the nun costume."

"Nun costume?" Rosie spluttered. "Emma, we're trying not to draw attention to ourselves!"

But her protests fell on deaf ears as the others descended on the costume bag like seagulls on a dropped ice cream cone. And so began preparations for the Great Richard Stakeout.

The next morning saw Rosie peering out of her front window once again, this time barely able to contain her laughter. There, pruning her rose bushes with more enthusiasm than skill, was Trisha. Or rather, a very unconvincing elderly gardener who bore a striking resemblance to Trisha in a grey wig and oversized dungarees.

"Yoo-hoo! Rosie, dear!" Trisha called out in a quavering voice that was probably meant to sound old. "Lovely day for a bit of gardening, isn't it?"

Rosie watched in a mixture of amusement and horror as Trisha proceeded to hack at her prized roses with the grace of a drunk lumberjack.

"Yes, lovely," she called back weakly. "Though perhaps the roses have had enough... pruning for one day?"

Trisha gave her an exaggerated wink that was visible from space. "Don't you worry, dearie. I've got my eyes peeled for any suspicious characters!"

She punctuated this statement by nearly taking off her finger with the secateurs.

As the day wore on, the parade of poorly disguised sexagenarians continued. Lisa took up a position as a very glamorous window cleaner, spending more time adjusting her silk headscarf than actually cleaning any windows. Julie set up an easel on the pavement and proceeded to paint what she claimed was "an abstract representation of suburban ennui" but looked suspiciously like a bunch of squiggles to Rosie's untrained eye.

But it was Emma's turn on watch that took the cake. As the sun began to set, she emerged from Rosie's house in full nun regalia, complete with a habit that looked like it had seen better days (possibly in the 15th century) and a rosary that, upon closer inspection, appeared to be made of wine corks.

"Good evening, my children," Emma intoned in a voice that was probably meant to be pious but came across more like she was auditioning for a particularly hammy production of The Sound of Music. "I'm just out for my evening constitutional. And to save a few souls, of course. Any sinners about?"

Mrs Fitzgerald from number 23, out walking her poodle, did a double-take so dramatic that she nearly garrotted herself with the dog lead.

"Emma," Rosie hissed from the doorway, "what on earth are you doing?"

"Keeping the peace, my child," Emma replied serenely, before ruining the effect by pulling a hip flask from somewhere within the folds of her habit and taking a hearty swig. "The Lord's work is thirsty business."

Rosie groaned, retreating into the house and wondering, not for the first time, how her life had come to this.

Inside, she found Catherine and Maria huddled around the kitchen table, poring over what appeared to be architectural plans.

"Um, what's all this?" Rosie asked, almost afraid of the answer.

Catherine looked up, her eyes shining with an almost

manic light. "We're planning escape routes! Look, if Richard comes in the front, we can shimmy down the drainpipe here, or if he tries the back door, there's a lovely big rhododendron we could hide in."

Maria nodded enthusiastically. "And I've been researching how to make smoke bombs out of household chemicals. You know, just in case we need a diversion."

Rosie pinched the bridge of her nose, feeling a headache coming on. "Ladies, don't you think this is all getting a bit... out of hand?"

But before either of them could respond, a shrill whistle pierced the air - the signal they'd agreed on to indicate Richard had been spotted.

"Battle stations!" Catherine yelped, upending her chair in her haste to get to the window. They all peered out to see Emma, still in full nun costume, facing off against a very confused-looking Richard on the pavement.

"Do not go near that woman, you fiend!" Emma was bellowing, waving her rosary like a weapon. "The power of Christ compels you!"

Richard, to his credit, looked utterly baffled. "I... what? Look, I just want to talk to Catherine. Who are you?"

"I am Sister Mary Merlot of the Order of Perpetual Sobriety," Emma declared. "And I'll not have you harassing these good women!"

By this point, a small crowd had begun to gather, drawn by the spectacle of a nun in hoop earrings berating a middle-aged man on a quiet suburban street.

"Oh god," Catherine moaned, burying her face in her hands. "This can't be happening."

But it was happening, and it was about to get worse. As Richard tried to sidestep Emma, she made a grab for him, missed, and instead managed to knock off her wimple.

"Emma?" Richard exclaimed, recognition dawning. "What on earth-"

But Emma, never one to admit defeat, doubled down. "The power of Chardonnay compels you!" she roared, splashing the contents of her hip flask at Richard. It was at this precise moment that a police car, summoned by a well-meaning but utterly confused neighbour, pulled up to the curb.

What followed was a scene of such sublime chaos that it would go down in neighbourhood legend for years to come. Emma, trying to flee, tripped over her habit and face-planted into Mrs. Fitzgerald's petunias. Richard, still spluttering from his impromptu wine baptism, attempted to explain to the increasingly bewildered police officers that he was not being attacked by a militant order of nuns.

Meanwhile, the rest of the Sensational Sixties Squad, alerted by the commotion, descended on the scene in their various ridiculous disguises. Julie, still clutching her paintbrush, managed to splatter half the gathered crowd with what she swore was "cerulean blue" but looked suspiciously like emulsion. Trisha, in her gardener get-up, began loudly lecturing the police on the importance of proper lawn maintenance. Rosie, Catherine, and Maria watched from the doorway, torn between horror and hysterical laughter.

"Should... should we do something?" Catherine asked weakly. Rosie shook her head, a giggle escaping despite her best efforts. "Honestly, I think we'd only make it worse at this point."

It took nearly an hour for the situation to be sorted out. By the time the police left, having extracted promises from both Richard and Emma to "keep the peace," the entire street was buzzing with excitement. Mrs Fitzgerald was overheard telling anyone who would listen that she always knew "that woman was a bad influence," while Mr Thompson from the corner house was demanding to know if there was a secret convent in the neighbourhood that no one had told him about.

As the impromptu audience dispersed, the Sensational Sixties Squad retreated to Rosie's living room, a motley crew of dishevelled disguises and sheepish grins.

"Well," Emma said, breaking the silence and absently picking petunia petals out of her hair, "I think we can safely say that Operation: Ditch the Dick was a rousing success."

Catherine, who had been sitting in stunned silence, suddenly burst into laughter. "Oh my god," she gasped between giggles, "did you see Richard's face? I thought his eyes were going to pop out of his head!"

"You know," Trisha mused, wiping tears of mirth from her eyes, "I don't think Richard will be bothering you again anytime soon, Catherine. He looked positively terrified."

Catherine nodded, a newfound confidence in her posture. "You're right. And even if he does... well, I know I've got the best defence squad a woman could ask for."

Rosie looked around at her friends. "You're all completely mad," she said fondly. As they settled in to dissect the events of the day, planning their next move (and vetoing Emma's suggestion of forming a permanent neighbourhood watch called "The Nunsense Patrol"), Emma pulled out a clipboard.

"On our now infamous spa night we vowed to avenge the behaviours of Richard and David. I think we can safely say that operation Dick'n'Dave has begun in earnest. We should all be very pleased with ourselves."

"Yes," said Lisa, cautiously.

"You sound unsure," said Emma. "Everything OK?"

"Yes, everything's fine. I suppose I get concerned when we're more focused on vengeance rather than building each other up and planning great things for the future...do you know what I mean? It feels very negative to be throwing all our efforts into the men."

"I agree," said Rosie. She turned to Catherine. "Dick face is out of your life now...what would you most like to do now he's finally been kicked to the kerb?"

"I've always wanted to see the Northern Lights," she mused, a dreamy look in her eyes. "Richard always said it was too cold and impractical, but now... well, who's to stop me?"

"Certainly not us," Lisa chimed in. "In fact, why don't we all go? Can you imagine the seven of us loose in Iceland?"

The idea was met with enthusiastic agreement, and soon they were all throwing out suggestions for a grand adventure.

"We could go dog sledging!" Julie exclaimed.

"Or soak in those gorgeous hot springs," Trisha added.

"Ooh, and sample the local vodka," Emma said, her eyes twinkling mischievously.

"Let's take a look at the options for going there," said Rosie. "We'll price it up and collate some options then we can work out who fancies it."

"Good plan, Miss Organised," said Emma. "Have you had time to think about what you're going to do about Derek? Any thoughts about whether to take him back or not?"

As Rosie was about to speak, the sound of a car door slamming right outside the window made them all freeze. It was as if the car was on the driveway. Catherine's face paled.

"You don't think..."

Rosie was on her feet in an instant, peering out through the curtains. In the glow of the streetlights, she could make out a familiar figure approaching the house.

"It's Richard," she hissed. Catherine dropped her head into her hands.

"I'll never get rid of him," she said. "He's always going to be there, in the background, watching me and interfering in everything I do. I'm just going to have to accept it."

"No you're not," said Rosie. "Absolutely not. I'm calling the police."

"Don't do that," said Catherine.

"Why? He's on my property. He's trespassing."

"OK, but let's go and talk to him first."

Rosie looked at Catherine. If she didn't take firm action against this nutter, this sort of behaviour would go on forever.

"Wait!" Maria called out, emerging from the kitchen with a tray. "I have an idea."

As Richard's knock sounded at the door, Rosie took a deep breath and opened it, flanked by her friends with their hands on their hips and angry looks on their faces.

Richard's jaw dropped at the sight before him - a group of women in their sixties staring at him with looks of steely determination.

"Richard," Rosie said calmly, "what can we do for you?"

He gaped for a moment, his eyes darting from Emma to Julie. "How many women live here? There are dozens of you," he said. "I just wanted to talk to Catherine."

"I'm afraid that's not possible," Rosie replied. "You see, we've asked you not to come here as politely as we can. The next step is a call to the police, the step after that is a restraining order."

"But she's my wife, I have every right to see her."

"No, she's your ex-wife and you have no right at all to see her."

"Richard, they're right. It's time for you to leave me alone. Our marriage is in the past. I've moved on, you need to as well."

They watched in silent triumph as Richard dropped his head and walked back to his car.

"Oh God, I feel really bad now," said Catherine. "Perhaps I should have asked him what he wanted."

"No," said Rosie. "We know what he wanted – to find out what you're doing here, and to try and keep tabs on you even though you got divorced many years ago. This is called 'being cruel to be kind'."

"I guess," said Catherine

"It's not even cruel, if you ask me," added Emma. "It's perfectly straightforward behaviour."

"And it's something to entertain the neighbours," said Rosie. "I don't think there have ever been so many comings and goings in this street. It must be very exciting for them all."

"Speaking of excitement," Maria chimed in. "I've been cooking and there's a tray of freshly baked cookies cooling in the kitchen. Anyone fancy one?"

As the evening wore on, fuelled by wine and Maria's cupcakes, the women found themselves sharing stories and dreams they'd long kept hidden. Catherine confessed her secret desire to learn pole dancing ("For fitness, of course!"), while Julie revealed her plan to create a series of nude portraits of local pensioners ("It's about celebrating the beauty of ageing!").

Rosie sat back, watching her friends with a warm glow in her chest. "How about you, Rosie?" "Well, I was just thinking that I don't really 'need' anything right now. I feel happier than I have for years. I love where I live, I've got great friends, a lovely daughter and two gorgeous grandchildren. I'm happy with my lot."

"What about Derek? Do you wish you were back with him?"

"To be honest, I sometimes do. We had such a good marriage for so long. I always thought he'd be the man I grew old with."

"But he was unfaithful," said Maria. "You can't go back after that."

"No, I know it seems strange, and when I first found out about his affair it was all very raw, and I was devastated, but as time's gone on, the pain's faded and my bruised ego has started to mend. I don't think of him as a philanderer now, but as a man who made a mistake."

"Christ, I'm livid with David," said Maria.

"Yes, and I was with Derek but – I don't know – I often think that life's too short. That all happened five years ago. I'm not desperately hoping that we end up back together or anything, but I do think of him with a lot of affection."

"But Mike," they chorused. Rosie laughed.

"Yes, he's nice too."

"He's a handsome doctor and he thinks the world of you."

"Yes, I know. But it's early days. Who knows what will happen."

"If you don't want him, can I have him?" asked Maria.

"Sure, yes – anyone who's single gets a go on him," said Rosie.

"Hooray!" shouted the women.

As the clock struck midnight, Emma raised her glass in a toast. "To the Sensational Sixties Squad," she declared. "May we always be a thorn in the side of ex-husbands and may we all get to have a go on Dr Mike."

"Hear, hear!" the others chorused, clinking their glasses together. As they began to tidy up, making plans for their next meetup, Rosie's mind drifted again to thoughts of Derek and Mike. She couldn't keep avoiding them forever.

It was about time she worked out what to do. But how was she supposed to do that? It wasn't just a question of choosing between two men but choosing between two lifestyles.

The quiet, dignified retirement she'd once envisioned, or a life full of chaos, friends, dates and takeaways.

The latter option was very appealing now which is why she'd started to favour Mike, but what of the future? What about when she was 70, or even 80? Would she want a house full of crazy women then?

As the last of her friends departed, Rosie stood in her doorway, watching them go. Emma linked arms with Trisha and was trying to teach her a bawdy sea shanty. Julie and Lisa were deep in discussion about the Chancellor of the Exchequer whose book Lisa might write.

"I just think you're amazing," said Julie, looking at Lisa with barely disguised adoration.

Rosie smiled to herself. "Good night, you gorgeous lot," she shouted before retreating into the warmth.

"POLITICAL AFFAIR"

Rosie's peaceful morning cuppa was rudely interrupted by a frantic pounding on her front door. Perhaps Richard had returned with a mariachi band, or David was looking to sue them for ABH after they pelted him with toilet rolls?

She approached the door cautiously, peeping through the spyhole.

Instead of Richard's hangdog expression, she was met with the sight of Lisa's perfectly coiffed hair, now resembling an electrocuted poodle.

Rosie flung open the door. "Lisa? What on earth—"

But Lisa was already barrelling past her, slamming the door shut and leaning against it as if expecting a battering ram to follow. "They know!" she gasped; eyes wild. "The press, they found out about Gerald!"

Rosie blinked, trying to process this information. "Gerald? Do you mean Gerald Fitzsimmons, Chancellor of the Exchequer? What about him? They know that you're writing his book? Is that so awful?"

Lisa groaned, sliding down the door to sit on the floor, her usually impeccable suit crumpled.

"We've been... seeing each other. Romantically. For months."

Rosie's jaw dropped.

"You've been having an affair with the Chancellor?"

"Well, when you say it like that, it sounds so tawdry," Lisa muttered. "I'm being followed everywhere by journalists. I'm on the bloody news."

Before Rosie could respond, her phone began to buzz incessantly. She glanced at the screen to see a barrage of messages from the rest of the Sensational Sixties Squad:

Emma: "Turn on the telly NOW! Channel 4!"

Julie: "Oh my god, Lisa's on the news!"

Trisha: "I knew that 'economic stimulus package' she kept talking about sounded suspicious!"

Maria: "Ladies, focus! We need to help her!"

"The girls all know," said Rosie. "What can we do to help? What do you need?"

Rosie fumbled for the remote, switching on the TV just in time to see a grainy photo of Lisa and a distinguished-looking man fill the screen.

The headline below screamed: "SHADOW CHANCELLOR'S SECRET SEXAGENARIAN SWEETHEART!"

"Oh, bugger," Rosie muttered.

Lisa whimpered from her position on the floor. "What am I going to do? There are reporters camped outside my house. I had to sneak out through Mrs. Higgins' garden."

No wonder her hair looked like that.

"Right," Rosie said, snapping into action. "First things first. Tea."

Ten minutes and two fortifying cups of Earl Grey later, Lisa had calmed down enough to explain the situation. She'd agreed to write his book because she admired him professionally, but she also did quite fancy him, and their meetings to discuss narrative flow and chapter structure had resulted in romance developing between them.

"He's not even married!" Lisa wailed. "We weren't doing anything wrong. But now the press is making it sound like I'm some kind of... of..."

"Cougar?" Rosie supplied helpfully.

Lisa glared at her. "I was going to say 'homewrecker,' but thank you for that delightful image."

Before Rosie could apologise, the doorbell rang. She opened it to find the rest of the Sensational Sixties Squad on her doorstep, each looking more frazzled than the last.

"We came as soon as we saw the news," Emma announced. "There's a hell of a lot of journalists out there. Did you know?"

"Yeah. I had an idea," said Lisa.

For the next hour, Rosie's living room became a war room.

"Does he not have any advisers? Can't they tell you what to do?"

"Nope. No one seems interested in my welfare at all. I knew this, of course. They just want to protect him from any fallout. No one gives a toss about the woman whose house is surrounded."

"We care," said Julie. "We all care a lot."

"I know," said Lisa. "I'm lucky to have such amazing friends. You're all wonderful. It's just disappointing that of all the advisers in the entire British government, not one person is interested in advising me.

"Actually, it's worse than that...not one person has given a second thought to me or that I am caught up in this as well."

"I remember when you wrote speeches for that famous actor and it was the same then," said Emma. "He had about

50 million people on speed dial and none of them were interested in you."

"You had an affair with a famous actor?"

"No, no. But it gave me an insight into what fame does to people and the power it has. I remember walking up to a door with him, people would rush to open it for him and then let it close in my face.

"We'd walk towards a taxi and the driver would take his bag and carry it while I was left struggling with fine. Fame is an odd thing...it attracts interest and help, money and hangers-on. People like being part of it. They're blinded by it."

As Lisa spoke, her phone rang. "It's him. Listen, I'll have to get this," she said.

The women stood still while Lisa muttered a succession of 'yes', 'no' and 'I don't know'. Eventually, she put the phone down and turned to them. "I need to get to the little layby near Esher station," she said.

"It's about a 10-minute walk," said Catherine to the astonishment of everyone.

"She can't walk down the street, there are about a dozen photographers outside," said Rosie. "We need a plan. We need to be like Cagney and Lacey."

"Oh my God, I loved that show," said Emma.

"Right. My car is parked behind the house. We can reach it by going through the back garden, but someone will need to distract them at the front," said Rosie. "I'll have to come round onto the main road and there's only one way to do that...it takes me right passed them. We need them to be otherwise occupied or they might spot me."

"Sure," said Emma. "We can think of ways to distract them."

Rosie should have known, in that moment, as they sat around the table and made a plan, that things were going to drift seamlessly from the ridiculous to the utterly absurd.

Ten minutes later, Rosie and Lisa were poised by the door leading out of the sitting room and into the garden. It was a small garden with a gate on the end which led out to a string of garages. Rosie never used her garage. When she and Derek had lived together it was a store for a wide range of tools that she never understood the use of and her husband never used. Now it was a store for all of his things that he didn't take when he left. She'd asked him to take it several times in the past, and now it just sat there, presumably damp, covered in mould and no use to anyone.

Her car was parked directly at the bottom of her garden… easy to slip into and unlikely to be spotted until they were on the main road and going past the media scrum.

She looked at Lisa. "OK?'

"Yes. Thanks so much for this."

"My pleasure," said Rosie. "I'll just check that everyone is in the right place and ready to go."

She moved from the kitchen through to the small sitting room at the front of the house and peeped out between the slants of the closed blinds.

Emma was crouched behind her hydrangeas, wearing oversized sunglasses and clutching a homemade smoke bomb that smelled suspiciously like vinegar and baking soda.

Lisa came crawling along the carpet behind Rosie, determined not to be seen.

"Are you sure about this smoke bomb thing?" she said to Lisa. "Is this going to work?"

"Of course it is," said Lisa. "Shall we go?"

They walked and crawled back through the house and ran down the garden to the car. Lisa climbed into the back and lay down with a pile of coats on top of her, while Rosie jumped into the driver's seat.

"Ready?"

"Yes, all covered up and ready when you are."

Rosie sent a message to the group. "All units, all units. Be aware. The principal is on the move. The principal is on the move."

She was quite enjoying all this. She was keen to help Lisa in any way she could but was also immensely enjoying acting as if she were a close protection officer assigned to royalty.

She heard Lisa giggle from the back seat. "You've been watching too many terrible American films," she said.

"Principal is moving her lips, principal is moving her lips," said Rosie, as they drove round the corner.

As they approached the house, Rosie saw the Sensational Sixties squad members emerge from their hiding places and hurl the homemade floury bombs at the journalists. Rosie kept driving. She wanted to skid around the corner Starsky and Hutch style, but knew that drawing attention to her little car and its precious cargo was the last thing she should be doing when the others were working so hard to distract the media.

As Rosie turned, she saw the clouds of floury smoke filling the air behind her. She drove on, now happy that they would make their rendezvous safely.

Meanwhile, there was chaos back in Rosie's garden. The reporters scattered in confusion. Cameras swung wildly, trying to capture the madness. Rosie's perfectly manicured lawn devolved into a battlefield.

In the middle of it all stood Emma, overjoyed by the carnage, thrilled that she'd been able to help her friend, and wondering whether they could get everything cleaned up and sorted out before Rosie returned.

The next few days passed in a blur of media frenzy. Rosie's house became the unofficial headquarters of "Operation: Save Lisa's Reputation" (Emma had wanted to call it "Operation: Hot for the Chancellor," but had been firmly vetoed).

They took turns fielding phone calls from reporters, each coming up with increasingly outlandish stories to throw them off the scent. "Lisa Worthington? Oh, you must mean my great-aunt Lisa," Rosie found herself telling one particularly persistent journalist. "Lovely woman, but a bit old now. She's lost touch with reality. Thinks she's having an affair with Winston Churchill's ghost. Sad, really."

It was on the third day of this madness that things came to a head. Rosie was in the middle of assuring a reporter that Lisa had joined a silent monastery in Tibet when she heard a huge commotion in the street. Peering through the curtains, she saw a sight that made her heart sink. There, striding up her garden path with the confidence of a man who'd never had to throw homemade bombs at reporters, was Gerald Fitzsimmons himself.

"Oh, blimey," Rosie muttered. She turned to the others, who were all frozen in various states of panic. "Ladies, we've got company. Important, political company."

Emma's eyes gleamed with mischief.

"I've got a plan," she said.

But there was no time, the doorbell rang, and Rosie stepped forward to answer it.

Gerald Fitzsimmons was every bit as distinguished in person as he appeared on TV. His silver hair was immaculately coiffed, his suit crisp despite the warm weather. He fixed Rosie with a penetrating gaze. "Mrs Brown, I presume?" he said, his voice smooth as silk while cameras clicked and flashed, and Rosie wished she were wearing something nicer.

"I believe you know where I might find Lisa Worthington."

Rosie opened her mouth, prepared to deny everything, when a voice from behind her said quietly, "It's alright, Rosie. Let him in."

Lisa stepped into view, looking more like herself than she

had in days. She'd borrowed one of Rosie's dresses, her hair was neatly styled, and there was a determined set to her jaw. As Gerald entered, the atmosphere in the room could have been cut with a knife.

The Sensational Sixties Squad watched with bated breath as Lisa and Gerald faced each other.

"Lisa," Gerald began, "I came to—"

But Lisa held up a hand, silencing him. "Before you say anything, Gerald, I want you to know that I don't regret a single moment of our time together. But I won't be your dirty little secret, hidden away while you play the respectable politician."

Gerald blinked, looking taken aback. "I... what? Lisa, I came here to ask you to marry me."

The room erupted in gasps. Emma dropped her coffee cup. Catherine, who had been stress-eating Maria's muffins, choked and had to be thumped on the back by Trisha.

Lisa stared at Gerald, her eyes wide. "Marry you? But... the press, your career..."

Gerald shook his head, a wry smile on his face. "Lisa, I'm the Chancellor of the Exchequer. Do you think I care what the tabloids say about my love life? Besides," he added with a chuckle, "my approval ratings have gone through the roof since this all came out. The public loves the idea of a politician who can balance the budget and still find time for romance."

Lisa's face broke into a radiant smile. "Oh, Gerald," she said, stepping into his arms.

Rosie felt a wave of emotion wash over her. She looked around at her friends – Emma pretending not to cry (and failing miserably), Julie already mentally sketching out designs for wedding centrepieces, Catherine and Maria hugging each other and jumping up and down like schoolgirls.

"Wait," shouted Lisa. "I haven't said anything."

The women stopped and stood still, waiting for the formal acceptance of the proposal.

"I'm sorry," said Lisa. "I love you, but I'm not ready to marry you."

Gerald looked crestfallen. The women didn't know where to look.

"Can we carry on seeing one another? I want to know you better before we get married. I don't have completely great memories of married life. I'd like us to proceed slowly."

"But if we got married it would look so much better," said Gerald.

Lisa looked at him. "It would look better?"

"No. That came out wrong. I mean that it would take the pressure off. There wouldn't be all this judgment from everyone."

"Yeah, because this is all about us making sure you're judged properly."

"No, Lisa. You're completely missing the point."

"OK. But the fact remains that I'm not ready to get married. Not yet."

Rosie slipped away to the kitchen to put the kettle on. Some occasions, after all, called for a proper cup of tea. She was just pouring the water when she heard a knock at the patio doors at the back of the house. If it was a journalist, she'd lose her mind.

They were filling the street at the front but so far hadn't trespassed on her back garden. She peeped through the closed shutters to see Mike standing there, a bemused expression on his face and a bouquet in his hand.

"Rosie," he said as he saw her peeping through. "Why's there a throng of photographers and a news van parked outside your house?"

Rosie opened the patio door and looked at Mike, took in

his twinkling eyes and the warm smile that made her heart flutter, and smiled.

"Come in," she said. As Mike kissed Rosie on the cheek and handed her the flowers, Gerald walked into the kitchen.

"Ah," said Mike. "Well, that answers one question, but it throws up a hell of a lot more."

"THE PUB PREDICAMENT"

※

        *R*osie smoothed down her blouse for the umpteenth time, scrutinising her reflection in the hallway mirror. She'd opted for a soft blue number that brought out her eyes, paired with jeans that she hoped made her look more "casually chic" than "desperately trying to recapture her youth."

"It's just a quiet drink with Mike," she muttered to herself. "Nothing to be nervous about."

Her phone buzzed with a message from Emma: "Go get 'em, tiger! And remember, if all else fails, you can always fake a heart attack. I'll be your alibi."

Rosie chuckled, shaking her head. Trust Emma to have a contingency plan that involves hospitalisation. She opened her front door and was immediately relieved to see that the news crews who'd been camped outside all week had finally gone on to report on something else. They didn't seem remotely interested in the fact that Rosie was going on a date with a handsome doctor.

She set out on the short walk to The Red Lion pub. With each step, Rosie's mind raced with potential scenarios. What if she spilled her drink? What if she had spinach in her teeth? What if Mike took one look at her and realised he'd rather date someone whose back didn't make alarming creaking noises every time she stood up?

As she approached the pub, she took a deep breath, squared her shoulders, and pushed open the door.

The familiar sounds and smells washed over her - the clinking of glasses, the murmur of conversation, the faint aroma of beer and decades-old carpet.

Scanning the room, she spotted Mike at a corner table, looking as handsome as ever in a crisp blue shirt. Her heart did a little flip as he caught her eye and smiled, raising his hand in greeting.

Rosie began to weave her way through the crowd, her confidence growing with each step. She could do this. She was a mature, sophisticated woman who- "Rosie? Is that you?" She froze. She knew that voice. Turning slowly, she came face to face with Derek, her estranged husband, looking as surprised to see her as she was to see him.

"Derek," she managed, her voice unnaturally high. "What a... surprise."

Derek smiled, that familiar grin that used to make her knees weak. She didn't feel the same about it now, it certainly didn't make her weak, but it made her feel warm and comforted. There was no doubt that Derek's familiarity was reassuring It was just badly timed.

"It's good to see you," he said, taking a step closer. "You look wonderful."

"Ah, yes, well," Rosie stammered, acutely aware of Mike watching from across the room. "Lovely to see you, too."

She turned to flee, only to find her escape route blocked by a group of rowdy football fans who'd just entered. Derek appeared behind her. She didn't know what to do, so she did the only sensible thing, the sort of thing that any mature, sophisticated woman would do - she ducked behind the bar so neither of them could see her.

"Can I help you?" the startled bartender yelped.

"Sorry. I'm having a bit of an emergency," Rosie hissed, crouching down among the kegs. "I'll explain later. Just... pretend I'm not here."

The bartender, a young man who looked like he'd seen his fair share of odd behaviour from the pub's patrons, shrugged and went back to pulling pints.

Rosie peered out from her hiding spot, assessing the situation. Derek was looking around in confusion, while Mike was half-rising from his seat, a concerned expression on his face. Presumably wondering how the women he'd just watched walking across the bar had now disappeared into thin air.

This was not how she'd envisioned her evening going.

"Rough night?" asked the barman, casually sliding her a glass of wine. Rosie accepted it gratefully.

"You have no idea," she sighed, taking a long sip. "I'm on a date with a man I've just met, and my husband is in the bar."

"Your husband?" "Yes – but not like that. We've been separated for years."

"Ah, I see."

From the other side of the bar, Rosie could hear football songs being sung… off-key lines about never walking alone, and lions on shirts were being belted out across the crowded bar.

"I'm not sure what to do…" she said to the young barman.

"What do you want to do?" he asked, crouching down next to her.

"Well, that's the problem," she said, sitting back on an old crate. "Part of me wants to go back to Derek because I understand that. Life is easier with someone you've known forever, but once that person lets you down it can be hard."

"So, your husband let you down?"

"He had an affair. With someone I know."

"Christ. That's awful. Forget about him and go for the new guy."

"Yes, I know – that's what all my friends are saying, but my husband and I have a daughter and two little granddaughters, and a lifetime of living together."

"Granddaughters?" said the barman. "How can you have granddaughters? You look about my age."

The barman looked about 30.

"That's very kind," she said. "But I think we both know that I'm about twice your age."

"I don't know about that. I was thinking how attractive you were." Rosie felt her cheeks colouring. Was he flirting with her? "Tell me about the other guy. The one you are supposed to be on a date with."

"He's nice," she said. "Handsome, bright and interesting. I like him a lot. He turned up at my house with flowers the other day. He's lovely. He's exactly my type, but I'm worried that the reason I'm not going for it with him is because I'm still in love with Derek."

"It sounds like you might be," said the barman. "Perhaps you should just play the field for a bit. Have fun with the new guy but don't take him too seriously."

"Yeah, I guess, but I don't want to mess him around."

"Don't worry about that. I'm sure he'll survive. Try and think about yourself. You've been through a lot."

"Matt," came a call from one of the barmaids. "There's someone here to see you."

The barman went to stand up, just as a man peered over the bar.

"Mike," said Rosie.

"Dad," said Matt.

They all looked from one to another as another head

appeared.

"Derek," said Rosie.

"That's your husband?" said Matt. "I see him here all the time."

"Whose husband?" asked Mike, while Rosie sank back down onto her crate and looked down at her hands.

The football fans continued their singing. The men above her were all looking down at her and all Rosie wished was that she was back in her house with her friends, drinking wine and having fun.

Sadly, despite fervent wishing, Rosie didn't find herself at home on the sofa, but flanked by Mike and Derek, both looking equal parts confused and intrigued.

"Rosie," Derek began, "Are you okay? Do you need help?"

"I'm fine. I'm just here to meet Mike for a drink."

"We're on a date," said Mike, aggressively.

"Oh, I see," said Derek, nodding slowly, a hint of sadness in his eyes. "I'm glad you're happy, Rosie. You deserve it."

With a final smile, he turned and walked away, leaving Rosie flooded with a barrage of feelings. She then turned to Mike, who was watching her with a twinkle in his eye.

"Mike," she began, "I'm so sorry about all this. I understand if you want to run for the hills. That was my husband, Derek, we separated years ago."

"I know. You mentioned him. He's one of my patients."

"Is he? That's awkward."

"It's fine. I'm a professional."

Matt had stayed silent during all the conversations, but he put his hand up as they chatted.

"Rosie thinks she might still be in love with her husband."

Rosie shrugged. What could she say? She'd just spoken at length to Matt about her dilemma.

"Is that true?" asked Mike.

"I don't know. I like you, and I'd love to carry on seeing you, but I do feel odd when Derek's around."

"Odd?"

"Yes. Full of memories about the past."

"Good memories?"

"Well, they haven't all been good – no – the guy had an affair, for God's sake, but hearing that he's single again has made me question myself. I want to be very sure I'm doing the right thing."

"I think we all feel a bit odd when we're confronted by our exes."

"Yes," said Mike. "If my ex lived anywhere near me I'd find it extremely difficult."

"Where does your ex live?"

"Mum lives in Wales," said Matt. "Not far from Cardiff."

"I'd still like us to go out for dinner tonight. If you want to?"

"Yes," said Rosie. "I'd like that very much."

"I'll just nip to the loo, then we can head off."

Once Mike was out of sight, Rise turned to Matt. "I'm sorry," she said. "I like your dad a lot. It just threw me having them both in the pub at the same time."

"I understand," said Matt. "But please don't hurt dad. Be honest with him."

"I promise I will."

"Interesting news that your boyfriend is your ex-husband's doctor."

Honestly, Matt. My world is bonkers right now, but that is insane."

* * *

LATER THAT NIGHT, having had a lovely meal with Rosie,

Mike paced the length of his living room, phone pressed to his ear.

"I'm telling you, Jack, it was like something out of a sitcom. There I was, watching her walk across the bar then she suddenly disappeared. No sign of her anywhere. I went over to talk to Matt and found her sitting on the floor. The two of them chatted away. She told him all about her husband turning up in the bar when she was on a date. What she didn't realise was that Matt was the date's son!"

Jack's laughter crackled through the phone. "Sounds like you're in for quite the ride with this one, mate. But the real question is - is she worth it?"

Mike paused his pacing, a smile softening his features. "She is. God help me, but she is. Rosie's... she's like a breath of fresh air. She makes me see the world differently, makes me want to embrace life the way she does."

"But?" Jack prompted, knowing his friend well enough to hear the unspoken concern. "But I can't help wondering if I'm setting myself up for heartbreak," Mike admitted. "Her ex-husband is still in the picture, and they have so much history..."

"Mike," Jack's voice turned serious, "in all the years I've known you, I've never heard you talk about a woman the way you talk about Rosie. Don't let fear hold you back. If she's worth it - and it sounds like she is - then she's worth the risk."

Mike took a deep breath, feeling some of the tension leave his shoulders. "You're right. Of course, you're right. Thanks, Jack. I needed to hear that."

As he hung up, Mike felt a renewed sense of determination. Yes, the situation with Rosie was complicated. Yes, there was a risk of getting hurt. But as he thought about her laugh, her zest for life, the way she made him feel... he knew Jack was right. Rosie was worth any risk.

"DECISIONS, DECISIONS"

Rosie stood in her kitchen, staring blankly at the kettle as if it might suddenly spring to life and offer sage advice. The events of the previous night at the pub swirled in her mind like a particularly chaotic tea leaves reading.

"Get a grip, Rosie," she muttered to herself, finally flicking on the kettle. "You're a grown woman, not a teenager trying to decide who to take to prom."

They'd had a lovely date the night before. After inauspicious beginnings, they had gone to the pretty Lebanese restaurant in Hampton Court, very near to where her daughter Mary lived.

The food, the wine and the company had all been great, and even though she had been incredibly embarrassed when Matt had told his father that Rosie's ex was in the bar, it had been great to discuss everything openly.

In some ways, the whole thing had brought Mike and her closer together.

As if summoned by the promise of tea and drama, the doorbell rang. Rosie opened it to find Emma on her doorstep. She'd texted Emma last night to update her on the whole bar situation.

"Morning, sunshine!" Emma chirped, breezing past Rosie into the house. "I brought reinforcements."

She held up a bag that clinked suspiciously. "Mimosa ingredients. It's five o'clock somewhere, right?"

Rosie raised an eyebrow. "It's 9 AM, Emma."

"Exactly. Prime mimosa time. Now, where do you keep your champagne flutes?"

Before Rosie could protest that she didn't, in fact, own champagne flutes (wine glasses from the local supermarket were more her speed), the doorbell rang again.

This time, it was Lisa, Catherine, and Julie, each bearing their contributions to what was apparently going to be an impromptu brunch.

"We thought you might want to talk about your hot date last night," Lisa explained, hefting a bag of groceries. "And possibly an intervention if Emma's already broken into the alcohol."

Soon, the kitchen was a hive of activity. Lisa had taken charge of cooking, wielding a spatula with the authority of a five-star chef.

Julie was arranging flowers in what she claimed was a "symbolic representation of Rosie's emotional journey," but looked suspiciously like she'd just grabbed whatever was still alive in Rosie's neglected garden.

Catherine was nervously rearranging the cutlery, occasionally shooting worried glances at Rosie as if expecting her to burst into tears at any moment.

And Emma, true to form, was mixing mimosas with the flair of a bartender and the heavy-handedness of... well, Emma.

"Right," Emma announced, placing a violently orange concoction in front of Rosie. "Drink up, darling. Nothing like a little liquid courage to kick-start the decision-making process."

Rosie eyed the drink warily. "Emma, I'm not sure getting sozzled before noon."

Emma waved a dismissive hand. "Nonsense. Some of my best decisions were made under the influence. Did I ever tell you about the time I decided to take up pole dancing? Granted, I couldn't walk properly for a week afterwards, but the paramedic was very handsome."

"Ladies," Lisa interrupted, placing a platter of what appeared to be gourmet avocado toast on the table, "perhaps we should focus on Rosie's dilemma. Derek or Mike?"

Rosie groaned, burying her face in her hands. "When you put it like that, I feel like I'm on some terrible reality dating show. 'The Sexagenarian Bachelorette.'"

"Ooh, I'd watch that," Julie piped up. "Imagine the cocktail parties. Instead of roses, you could hand out... I don't know, reading glasses?"

"Or tubes of arthritis cream," Catherine added, warming to the theme.

As her friends dissolved into giggles, Lisa fought to instil some order. "Alright, alright. Let's approach this logically. Rosie, why don't you tell us how you feel about Derek?"

Rosie took a sip of her mimosa (which was, predictably, about 90% champagne) and considered the question.

"Derek... well, there's history there. Thirty years of marriage, raising Mary together. He knows me better than anyone."

"But?" Emma prompted.

"But," Rosie continued, "when I think about going back to that life... it feels like putting on an old sweater. Comfortable, familiar, but maybe not quite the right fit anymore."

Her friends nodded encouragingly.

"And Mike?" Catherine asked gently.

Rosie felt a smile tugging at her lips. "Mike is... he's unexpected. He makes me feel like I'm discovering parts of myself I didn't even know existed. But it's also scary. Starting something new at our age..."

"Oh, pish posh," Emma interjected. "Age is just a number. And in our case, it's a number that comes with a free bus pass and excellent discounts at garden centres."

This set off another round of laughter, but Rosie appreciated the sentiment behind Emma's words.

"The thing is," Rosie continued, "it's not just about choosing between Derek and Mike. It's about choosing who I want to be at this stage of my life."

Lisa nodded sagely. "That's very insightful, Rosie. So, who do you want to be?"

Rosie stood up, pacing the kitchen as she tried to articulate the thoughts that had been swirling in her mind. "I want to be someone who isn't afraid to take risks. Someone who embraces new experiences. I want to be the kind of woman who... who joins a salsa class on a whim, or decides to learn Mandarin just because she can."

"That's the spirit!" Emma cheered, raising her mimosa glass. "Live a little! Or in our case, live a lot in whatever time we've got left before our hips give out entirely."

Rosie continued, warming to her theme. "When I was with Derek, I was always somebody's wife, somebody's mother. And those are important parts of who I am, but they're not all of me. These past few months, being with you lot," she gestured to her friends, "I've remembered that I'm also just Rosie. And I like her. I like who I am when I'm not trying to fit into someone else's idea of who I should be."

There was a moment of silence as her words sank in. Then Julie spoke up, her voice uncharacteristically serious. "Rosie, my dear, I think you've just made your decision."

Rosie blinked, realising Julie was right. Somehow, in

trying to explain her feelings to her friends, she'd clarified them for herself as well. "I have, haven't I?" she said, a sense of relief washing over her. "I'm not going back to Derek. I'm moving forward."

The kitchen erupted in cheers. Emma, in her enthusiasm, knocked over her mimosa, creating a sticky orange puddle on the table. "Oh, botheration," Emma muttered, attempting to mop up the spill with what turned out to be one of Julie's "artistic" napkin creations.

"Sorry about that. But more importantly - Rosie! Our girl's choosing adventure over arthritis cream! This calls for more champagne!"

As Emma bustled about, replenishing glasses and narrowly avoiding setting her sleeve on fire with the toaster, Lisa turned to Rosie with a warm smile.

"I'm proud of you, Rosie. It takes courage to choose the unknown over the familiar."

Rosie felt a lump form in her throat. "Thank you," she said softly. "I couldn't have done it without all of you. You've shown me that life doesn't end at sixty. It just... gets more interesting."

"And how!" Catherine chimed in. "Why, just last week I learned how to use the 'Snap Filter' thing on my phone. Did you know you can make yourself look like a cat? Technology these days, I tell you!"

As her friends laughed and began sharing their own recent "adventures" Rosie felt a weight lift from her shoulders. The decision she'd been agonising over suddenly seemed so clear.

"Right," she announced, raising her glass. "I propose a toast. To new beginnings, old friends, and the adventures yet to come."

"Here, here!" her friends chorused, clinking glasses with more enthusiasm than coordination. As they settled in to enjoy their brunch, the conversation flowing as freely as Emma's heavy-handed mimosas, Rosie found herself imagining the possibilities that lay ahead. Maybe she would take that salsa class. Or perhaps she'd finally write that novel she'd been thinking about for years. And yes, maybe she'd see where things went with Mike. The future stretched out before her, not as a well-worn path, but as an open road full of potential. It was exciting. It was terrifying. It was exactly what she needed.

Later that afternoon, as her friends were preparing to leave (Emma insisting she was perfectly fine to drive, despite walking into the coat rack twice and addressing it as "Madam President"), Rosie pulled each of them aside for a heartfelt thank you.

To Lisa, she said, "Thank you for always being the voice of reason. Even when reason seems to have gone on holiday and left chaos in charge."

Lisa chuckled, pulling Rosie into a warm hug. "That's what friends are for. Besides, someone has to keep Emma from turning every situation into a Shakespearean drama. Or a Monty Python sketch, depending on her mood."

To Catherine, Rosie expressed her gratitude for her unwavering support. "You've shown me that it's never too late to stand up for yourself and what you want."

Catherine beamed, her eyes misty. "Oh, Rosie. You've done the same for me. Who would have thought we'd be starting new chapters in our lives at our age? It's terrifying and wonderful, isn't it?"

Julie received thanks for her artistic spirit and ability to find beauty in the everyday. "You've reminded me to look at the world with fresh eyes," Rosie told her.

Julie responded by presenting Rosie with a hastily sketched portrait of their brunch, which seemed to feature Emma as some sort of mimosa-wielding superhero.

"I call it 'Sisterhood of the Travelling Spanx,'" Julie announced proudly.

And finally, to Emma, Rosie simply said, "Thank you for being you. Unabashedly, unapologetically you."

Emma, in a rare moment of seriousness, took Rosie's hands in hers.

"Rosie, my dear, you don't need to thank me. But if you insist, you can repay me by living your life to the fullest. Take chances. Make mistakes. Get messy. And for god's sake, buy some proper champagne flutes. We're not barbarians."

As the last of her friends departed, leaving behind a kitchen that looked like it had hosted a particularly rowdy toddlers' birthday party. Rosie sank onto her sofa with a contented sigh.

She pulled out her phone, staring at Derek's number for a long moment. Then, with a decisive nod, she began to type:

"Derek, we need to talk. Not about reconciliation, but about moving forward. Separately. I've realised that I'm not the same woman I was when we were married. I've changed, and grown, and I want to explore who I am now.

"I hope you can understand and respect my decision. Perhaps we can meet for coffee soon to discuss things calmly. Take care, Rosie."

Her finger hovered over the send button for just a moment before she pressed it firmly.

As the "message sent" notification appeared, Rosie felt a curious mix of sadness and liberation.

* * *

ACROSS TOWN, Derek stared at the message on his phone. He'd laid his heart bare to Rosie, hoping for a second chance. He thought of Rosie as he'd last seen her – vibrant, confident, surrounded by friends who brought out a side of her he'd never known existed. And he thought of himself – stuck in the past, hoping to reclaim something that had already evolved beyond his grasp.

"She's moved on," he whispered to the empty room.

The truth of it hit him like a physical blow. Rosie, his Rosie, had found a life without him. A life that, he had to admit, seemed to suit her far better than the one they'd shared.

He would beg her to come to counselling with him and he would do everything he could to keep the marriage together but, deep down, he knew it was over.

* * *

Rosie's hand was trembling. She shouldn't have sent a message, she should have called him, but she knew she couldn't. He'd persuade her to stay and she wouldn't be able to hurt him.

She watched the two blue ticks appear. He was reading it now. She scrolled to Mike's number before she lost her nerve and typed another message:

"Hi Mike. Sorry about the chaos at the pub. Turns out life can be quite an adventure, even (especially?) at our age. Fancy joining me for a proper date soon? No hiding behind the bar with your son this time. Let's talk properly. I've come to some major decisions. Let me know. Rosie."

As she set her phone down, Rosie looked around her living room. The same familiar walls and furniture surrounded her, but somehow everything looked different. Brighter. Full of possibility.

She stood up, walking to the window and gazing out at the street where she'd lived for so many years. The same trees, the same houses, the same neighbours walking their dogs. But now, instead of seeing a static, unchanging world, she saw potential adventures around every corner.

"Well, Rosie," she said to herself, a smile playing on her lips, "looks like life's about to get interesting."

And with that, she turned away from the window and began tidying up the kitchen, humming a tune that sounded suspiciously like "I Will Survive." Because really, what better anthem could there be for a woman embracing her second act?

As she wiped down the counter, her phone buzzed. A reply from Mike: "Rosie, I'd be delighted. How about Saturday? I know a great little jazz club in Kingston. Looking forward to it. Mike."

Rosie grinned, her heart doing a little flip that had nothing to do with her earlier mimosa consumption.

"TODDLER TWINS"

~~~~

*R*osie's peaceful morning was interrupted by the sound of her doorbell,

"Coming!" she called, hurrying to the door. She opened it to find her daughter Mary on the doorstep, looking rather frazzled. Her hair was escaping its ponytail, and she was juggling two backpacks and a tote bag overflowing with snacks and toys.

"Mum," Mary said, her voice a mix of desperation and relief. "You're a lifesaver. Are you sure you're okay with this? It's just for a few hours, I promise. Ted can't get off work, and I have this important meeting, and..."

"It's fine," Rosie interrupted, reaching out to take the bags. "How hard can it be? I raised you, after all."

Mary let out a slightly hysterical laugh. "Oh, Mum. You have no idea."

As Mary rushed off, leaving behind a trail of half-finished instructions and hurried kisses, Rosie found herself alone with her grandchildren.

She looked down at the two cherubic faces staring up at her. "Well," she said brightly, "this should be fun, shouldn't it?"

George and Daisy exchanged a mischievous glance that made Rosie wonder if she'd bitten off more than she could chew.

"Grandma," George said, his eyes wide with innocence, "can we build a rocket ship?"

"A rocket ship?" Rosie echoed, bemused.

Daisy nodded enthusiastically. "To fly to the moon and have tea with the aliens!"

Rosie chuckled. "Well, I'm not sure about the moon, but we could certainly build a lovely fort right here in the living room. How does that sound?"

The twins considered this for a moment before nodding in unison. "Okay," said Daisy.

"But can it be a space fort?" added George.

The boy had been obsessed with space since a trip to the science museum.

"Of course," Rosie agreed, already wondering how on earth she was going to manage this. In a moment of foresight, she did the only sensible thing - she called for reinforcements. Twenty minutes later, her living room looked like a whirlwind had torn through a toy shop and a NASA supply closet.

Emma was constructing an elaborate fort out of sofa cushions, blankets, and what appeared to be several colanders repurposed as space helmets.

"You know," Emma said, her voice muffled as she struggled to drape a sheet over a precarious tower of cushions, "I once dated an astronaut. Or was it an astrologer? Either way, he was very into stars."

Lisa was consulting a Google document called "Modern Approaches to Child Psychology," and muttering about "fostering creativity through imaginative play" and "the importance of adult participation in fantasy scenarios."

Julie had set up her easel and was trying to engage Daisy

in painting a mural of their imaginary space adventure. More paint seemed to be ending up on Daisy's overalls than on the paper, but the little girl was beaming with pride at her colourful creation.

Catherine, meanwhile, was attempting to interest George in a documentary about the solar system, which had worked for approximately thirty seconds before he decided that using the remote control as a "space blaster" was far more entertaining.

"I'm not sure Brian Cox is appropriate for three-year-olds," Rosie said doubtfully, watching as George zapped imaginary aliens with sound effects that would put any sci-fi movie to shame.

"Nonsense," Catherine replied. "It's never too early to appreciate the wonders of the cosmos. Besides, he seems to be enjoying it... in his way."

Indeed, George was now engaged in what appeared to be a very serious debate with an imaginary alien life form about the merits of having three heads versus just one.

As the morning wore on, the Sensational Sixties Squad found themselves facing challenges they'd never anticipated. Snack time turned into a strategic operation, with Lisa coordinating their efforts like a general planning a military campaign.

"Julie, offer the 'moon rocks' (cheese cubes)! Emma, stand by with the 'cosmic dust' (crushed crackers)! Catherine, be prepared with the 'alien smoothies' (green juice) if negotiations fail.

And for heaven's sake, someone distract them from the 'forbidden planet' (the biscuit tin)!"

Rosie watched in equal parts amusement and admiration as her friends transformed into a well-oiled (if slightly bewildered) childcare machine. She had to admit, they were nothing if not enthusiastic.

"You know," Julie mused as she attempted to convince Daisy that painting on paper was more fun than painting on her leg, "this reminds me of the time I tried to teach art to a group of particularly spirited pensioners. Same level of creativity, slightly less mess... actually, about the same level of mess."

Emma snorted. "Speak for yourself. I'm one crayon stain away from turning this shirt into an avant-garde masterpiece. Maybe I'll call it 'Supernova in Polyester' and sell it for millions."

As lunchtime approached, Rosie decided it was time for a walk in the park. Surely, she thought, fresh air would burn off some of the twins' seemingly endless energy. The simple act of getting two three-year-olds, five sixty-something women, and what seemed like half a toy shop's worth of entertainment out of the house and down the street turned into an expedition worthy of National Geographic.

"Emma, you can't bring a kite to the park," Rosie sighed, watching her friend attempt to stuff the oversized toy into an already bulging backpack.

"Why not?" Emma protested. "You never know when you might need an emergency distraction. Besides, it doubles as a makeshift sunshade. Or a sail, if we decide to commandeer a boat and become pirates instead of astronauts."

Eventually, they made it to the park, looking like a particularly eclectic tour group. Julie insisted on bringing her sketchpad ("The children's unbridled joy is simply begging to be captured!"). As they settled on a picnic blanket, attracting curious glances from other park-goers, Rosie felt a moment of pure contentment. Yes, it was chaotic. Yes, there was a very real possibility that one of them (probably Emma) might accidentally teach the twins something inappropriate. But looking around at her friends, all engaged in various games and activities with George and Daisy, she felt a warmth in her heart. Of course, the moment of peace didn't last long.

"Um, Rosie?" Catherine's voice was filled with concern. "Is it normal for children to try and climb trees at this age?"

Rosie whirled around to see George halfway up an oak tree, with Daisy cheering him on from below.

"Oh, for heaven's sake," she muttered, rushing over to coax him down. "George, darling, we don't climb trees without a grown-up to help us. We're not monkeys."

"But Grandma," George protested, his little face serious, "I'm not a monkey. I'm a brave space explorer looking for new planets!"

"Well, brave space explorer," Rosie said, trying to keep the amusement out of her voice, "I think this mission needs to be grounded for now. How about we explore the sandbox instead?"

As she helped George down, she could hear Emma chuckling behind her.

"You know," Emma mused, "it would make keeping an eye on them a lot easier if they were monkeys. Just give them some bananas and let them swing from the tree..."

But she was cut off by a sudden shriek from Julie.

"It's him, look. Richard. Down there by the river."

They all looked up to see Catherine's ex-husband running away.

"We've seen you," Julie shouted. "We're calling the Police."

But he'd gone. Disappeared into the park.

"We need to do something about him," said Rosie. "I've seen him a few times now, and though he's not bothering Catherine, he really shouldn't be hanging around us all the time."

"We'll make a plan," said Rosie. "We'll think of some way of making him leave us alone."

While they chatted, a small commotion was starting

around Julie's easel. They heard their friend wail and shout: "My masterpiece!" as she dived forward to save her painting that was flying off through the air.

In her haste, Julie knocked over the snack bag, sending its contents scattering across the grass. What followed was a scene of such delightful chaos that several nearby dog walkers stopped to watch, clearly unsure whether they were witnessing a unique childcare approach or a very strange performance art piece.

Emma, in a misguided attempt to help, began chasing after rolling apples, her progress hampered by the fact that she was now wearing the kite as a makeshift cape. "Fear not, citizens!" she called out dramatically. "Captain Kite is here to save the day!"

George and Daisy, delighted by this new game, began running after her, shouting "Save the apples! Save the apples!" at the top of their lungs.

Catherine, panicking at the sight of the twins gleefully helping themselves to the spilt snacks. "Now, children," she said, trying to sound stern but failing miserably, "we mustn't eat food off the ground. It's... it's not proper space explorer behaviour!"

Lisa, who'd been on the sidelines reading for most of the afternoon, abandoned her book and tried to distract the children with an impromptu puppet show using her reading glasses and a particularly expressive napkin.

"Look," she said, waving the napkin dramatically, "it's the... er... the Great Space Napkin! He's come to teach us about the importance of tidiness in zero gravity!"

In the middle of it all was Rosie, alternating between laughter and near tears, wondering how on earth Mary managed this every day.

Just as it seemed things couldn't get any more chaotic, a gust of wind caught Julie's abandoned sketch, sending it sailing across the park. Without thinking, Rosie took off after it, leaving the twins in the care of her friends (a decision she would immediately question).

She chased the paper across the grass, dodging startled picnickers and overenthusiastic dogs, all while yelling apologies over her shoulder.

"Sorry! Runaway art! Mind your heads!" Finally, with a leap that would have made an Olympic long jumper proud, she caught the sketch, tumbling to the ground in a tangle of limbs and grass stains.

As she lay there, catching her breath and wondering if sixty-something-year-old knees were supposed to bend that way, she heard a familiar voice.

"Rosie? Are you alright?" She looked up to see Mike standing over her, concern etched on his handsome face.

Of course, she thought. Of course, the universe would make sure the man she was interested in would see her like this - covered in grass stains and what she strongly suspected was a squashed banana, with a crayon-drawn flower adorning her cheek (courtesy of Daisy's earlier artistic endeavours).

"Oh, hello Mike," she said, trying to sound casual, as if sprawling on the ground in a public park was a perfectly normal way to spend a Tuesday afternoon.

"Lovely day, isn't it?"

Mike's concerned expression melted into an amused smile. "It certainly seems eventful," he said, offering her a hand up. "Dare I ask what's going on?"

Rosie accepted his help, wincing slightly as her knees protested the movement.

"Oh, you know," she said airily, "just a typical day out with the grandchildren and the girls. Nothing out of the ordinary."

As if on cue, a chorus of shrieks erupted from their picnic spot. Rosie turned to see Emma running across the grass, still wearing her kite cape, pursued by an angry-looking goose.

George was gleefully waving what appeared to be half of a sandwich, shouting "Look, Grandma! I'm feeding the space ducks!", while Daisy had somehow managed to cover herself head to toe in Julie's paints and was declaring herself the "Queen of the Colour Planet."

"I see," Mike said, his eyes twinkling with mirth. "Just a quiet day in the park, then?"

Rosie couldn't help but laugh. "Welcome to my world," she said. "Care to join the madness?"

To her surprise and delight, Mike nodded. "I'd be honoured," he said. "Though I should warn you, my child-wrangling skills are a bit rusty."

"Don't worry," Rosie assured him as they made their way back to the group. "Compared to this lot, you'll look like a professional."

The addition of Mike to their merry band seemed to bring a semblance of order to the chaos. He had a knack for engaging the twins and even managed to negotiate a truce between Emma and the aggrieved goose.

"You see, George," Mike was saying, crouched down to the little boy's level, "geese are a bit like the grumpy old aliens in your space stories. They're not really mean, they're just a bit misunderstood. And sometimes, they get scared when people run at them with big flappy things."

He shot a pointed look at Emma, who had the grace to look slightly abashed as she folded up her kite cape. As the afternoon wore on, the park became their playground. Mike organised a game of "Cosmic Hide and Seek," with the adults taking turns being the "Space Commander" searching for the hidden "alien life forms" (George and Daisy, giggling behind trees and bushes).

Julie set up an outdoor art class, teaching the twins how to make leaf rubbings and turn them into "alien landscapes."

Lisa, much to everyone's surprise, turned out to be an excellent storyteller, keeping the children spellbound with tales of friendly aliens and their adventures across the galaxy.

Even Catherine got into the spirit of things, leading an impromptu nature walk where every stick became a "laser blaster" and every interesting rock a "precious alien artefact."

As the sun began to set, casting a golden glow over the park, Rosie looked around at her unlikely family. Lisa was engrossed in a serious discussion with George about the aerodynamics of paper aeroplanes, her earlier rigidity softened by the child's earnest questions.

Julie had abandoned her painting in favour of creating daisy chains with Daisy, who was wearing them as royal regalia, declaring herself "Princess of the Flower Galaxy."

Catherine had dozed off on the picnic blanket, one protective arm draped over the twins' backpacks, a half-eaten biscuit still clutched in her hand.

Mike was sitting cross-legged on the grass, George and Daisy on either side of him, all three gazing up at the sky as he pointed out the stars, weaving a tale about each one.

And Emma... well, Emma was attempting to teach a group of fascinated children the finer points of cloud-watching, spinning tales of cloud dragons and cotton candy castles.

"Alright, you little dreamers," Rosie heard her say, "the secret is in the imagination. What do you see up there?"

As if sensing her gaze, Mike looked up and caught Rosie's eye. The warmth in his smile made her heart skip a beat.

"Quite a family you've got here," he said softly.

Rosie nodded, feeling a lump form in her throat. "They're a bit mad," she said. "But I wouldn't have them any other way."

Minutes later, Mary's car pulled up to the kerb. She got

out, looking significantly more put-together than she had that morning, and surveyed the scene before her with a mix of amusement and confusion.

Ted climbed out of the car, too, and rushed over to greet his daughters. The park was alive with the sounds of children playing and dogs barking.

Rosie and Mike stood up and walked hand in hand towards her daughter. Mary's gaze flicked curiously between Rosie and Mike.

"Mary, this is Mike," Rosie said, unable to keep the pride out of her voice.

"Mike, this is my daughter Mary and my son-in-law, Ted."

Mike stepped forward, his smile warm and genuine. "It's a pleasure to meet you, Mary. I've heard so much about you."

Mary's initial reserve seemed to melt away as she shook Mike's hand.

"I'll just go and say hello to Ted," he said, walking over to the car, where Ted was attempting to move the double pushchair out of the way so he could fit in all the rest of the paraphernalia.

"Let me help," said Mike, taking the pushchair so that Ted could load the boot. Behind them, Mary shot her mother an approving look.

Rosie felt her heart swell with happiness. Seeing Mike interact so naturally with her family felt right in a way she hadn't expected.

"So, Mike," Mary said, raising her voice, a mischievous glint in her eye, "I hope you know what you're getting into with Mum and her Sensational Sixties Squad. They're quite the handful."

Mike laughed, standing up to wrapping an arm around Rosie's waist.

"Oh, I think I can handle it. In fact, I'm rather looking forward to the adventure."

As Mike and Ted packed the last of the clothes, snacks and toys into the car, Rosie felt a deep sense of contentment wash over her.

Yes, the day had been chaotic.

Yes, there was a very real possibility that she'd be finding grass stains and stray crayons in her handbag for weeks to come.

But it had also been filled with laughter, love, and the kind of memories that would keep her warm on even the coldest nights. And Mary had met Mike…that was a huge hurdle navigated.

"Same time next week?" Emma asked hopefully as they said their goodbyes.

Mary's eyes widened in alarm, but Rosie just smiled. "Absolutely," she said. "Though perhaps we'll stick to indoor activities next time. I'm not sure the local goose population could handle another Emma encounter."

As she watched her friends disperse, each heading home with stories to tell and grass stains to scrub out, Rosie turned to Mike.

"Think you can handle the excitement of it all?"

"Oh yes," he replied. "Very much so."

* * *

DEREK'S KITCHEN WAS SPOTLESS, a stark contrast to the chaos of family life he'd left behind.

He placed a cup of tea in front of Mary, trying not to let his anxiety show.

"So," he began, aiming for casual and missing by a mile, "your mother seems... happy."

Mary nodded, wrapping her hands around the warm mug.

"She is, Dad. Happier than I've seen her in a long time."

Derek felt a pang in his chest. "And this Mike fellow... what's he like? Is he treating her well?"

Mary studied her father's face, noting the mix of concern and regret in his eyes. She took a deep breath, deciding honesty was the best policy.

"He's a nice guy, Dad," she said gently. "Kind, funny, and he adores Mum. The twins love him too."

Derek nodded, his expression a mixture of relief and sadness.

"Good. That's... that's good. Your mother deserves someone who makes her happy."

Mary reached out, placing her hand over her father's.

"Dad, I know this is hard for you. But Mum's in a good place now. Maybe it's time for you to think about moving forward too?"

Derek managed a weak smile. "You're right, of course. It's just... seeing her so happy without me, it's a bit of a kick in the teeth."

"I know," Mary said softly. "I know."

TED V MIKE

Ted paced the living room, his face set in a determined frown.

"I'm telling you, Mary, I need to meet this bloke. Your mum's been through enough. We can't just let any Tom, Dick, or Harry sweep her off her feet."

Mary rolled her eyes. "You met him in the park. Why the sudden need to interrogate him?"

"I'm not going to interrogate him, I'm going to check him out properly."

"You've already checked him out."

"No, he came to help me load things into the car. He was trying too hard."

"Trying too hard?"

"Yes. Any guy that tries too hard to be liked is trouble."

"So if he hadn't helped you to load things into the car, you'd have been happier?"

"No, of course not. I'd have been furious."

"So Mike couldn't win."

"Nope."

"This is crazy."

"He might be after her money, or he might upset her. I need to know exactly who we're dealing with."

"Mike's a doctor, Ted, not some con artist. Besides, Mum's a grown woman. She can make her own decisions."

"Still," Ted insisted, "it's my duty as her son-in-law. I'm going to invite him out for a pint. Man to man."

Mary sighed, knowing there was no deterring Ted when he got like this.

"Fine, but promise me you'll be nice."

"I can't promise," said Ted. "I might end up having a stern word with him."

The pub was crowded, the air thick with the smell of beer and the sound of football fans cheering at a match on the telly.

Ted sat rigidly at a corner table, his eyes fixed on the door. When Mike walked in, Ted's frown deepened. The man looked annoyingly presentable in his casual jumper and jeans.

"Ted?" Mike approached, hand outstretched. "It's great to see you again."

Ted grunted, shaking Mike's hand perhaps a bit too firmly. "Let's get a pint, shall we?"

As the evening wore on, Ted found his resolve weakening. Mike, it turned out, was not only a decent bloke but also a fellow football fan.

Their discussion of last season's matches grew increasingly animated.

"I'm telling you," Ted slurred slightly, gesticulating with his fifth (or was it sixth?) pint, "that referee needs his eyes checked!"

Mike nodded enthusiastically; his cheeks flushed. "Criminal, that call was. I was there. It was bloody ridiculous."

Hours flew by, filled with laughter, shared stories, and a growing camaraderie.

By closing time, Ted had an arm slung around Mike's shoulders as they attempted to sing a rather off-key rendition of their team's anthem.

"You know what, Mike?" Ted said as they stumbled out of the pub. "You're alright. Rosie's lucky to have you."

Mike grinned, looking both pleased and a bit wobbly. "Thanks, mate. I'm the lucky one, though. Rosie's amazing. And so's her family," he added, giving Ted a friendly punch on the arm that nearly sent them both toppling.

As they waited for their taxi, Ted's expression turned serious. "Just... take care of her, yeah? She deserves the best."

Mike nodded, his eyes sincere despite the alcohol-induced haze. "I promise, Ted. I'll do right by her."

The next morning, nursing spectacular hangovers, both men received the same text from Mary: "I hope you're both happy. Mum's insisting on hosting a family dinner next week. Something about 'her two favourite men becoming best mates.' What on earth did you two get up to last night?"

"RICHARD'S LAST STAND"

*R*osie peered out from behind her living room curtains for the umpteenth time that morning, her eyes narrowed as she scanned the quiet suburban street.

To the casual observer, it was a perfectly ordinary Wednesday. But Rosie knew better. Somewhere out there, lurking behind a hedge or possibly in a parked car, was Richard.

They knew this because his vehicle had been spotted at the back of Rosie's house earlier that day. And it wasn't the first time. Since they had bumped into him at the park with the twins, he'd been back in full stalking mode.

They'd spotted him in lots of places but hadn't got close enough to tell him what they thought, or alert the police to his presence.

"Any sign of him?" Catherine's voice sounded anxious. Rosie shook her head, letting the curtain fall back into place. "Not yet. But if he's out there, we'll call the police. We should have done so ages ago."

"He's there. I can feel it in my bones," said Catherine, wringing her hands. It had been two weeks since Richard's behaviour had escalated from the occasional drive-by to more persistent surveillance.

He'd been spotted peering through windows and lingering in the neighbourhood far too often for comfort.

"I still can't believe he followed me to my book club," Catherine moaned, collapsing onto the sofa. "Who does that? I mean, what did he think I was going to do? Run off with Mr. Darcy?"

Emma, who had been pacing the room like a caged tiger, snorted. "Well, to be fair, that Colin Firth does have a rather impressive... presence on screen."

Julie, who had been sketching furiously in the corner, looked up from her pad. "You know, this whole situation is quite thought-provoking. I'm thinking of doing a series called 'Love and Loss in Later Life.' Too melancholic?"

Before anyone could respond, the doorbell rang, making them all jump. Rosie approached it cautiously, half-expecting to find Richard on the other side with a bouquet and a poorly thought-out apology.

Instead, she opened the door to find Trisha, looking uncharacteristically frazzled.

"Ladies," Trisha announced, sweeping into the room with the air of someone about to unveil a particularly brilliant plan, "I've had an idea."

Emma perked up. "Ooh, is it the kind of idea that involves a nice glass of wine? Because I've got a lovely Bordeaux I've been saving for a special occasion."

Trisha waved away Emma's suggestion. "No, no. Well, maybe later. But first, I think I've figured out how we're going to solve our Richard problem once and for all."

The room fell silent as they all leaned in, eager to hear Trisha's plan.

Even Julie paused in her sketching, her pencil hovering expectantly over the paper.

"We're going to set up a situation where we can confront him directly in public, so he's embarrassed," Trisha declared, her eyes glinting with determination.

What followed was a planning session that would have put most diplomats to shame. The living room was transformed into a strategy room, with Julie's artistic skills put to use creating an elaborate map of the neighbourhood.

Emma, in a stroke of inspiration, suggested using her collection of colourful fridge magnets as markers for key locations.

"This little teapot magnet can represent the café where Catherine usually has her morning coffee," Emma explained, placing it on the makeshift map. "It's where Richard often 'coincidentally' shows up."

As the plan took shape, Rosie found herself marvelling at the creativity and resolve of her friends. The strategy, as Trisha outlined it, involved a fake outing for Catherine, a series of lookouts positioned around the neighbourhood, and what Emma enthusiastically referred to as

"Operation: Confront and Closure."

"Are we sure this is the best approach?" Lisa asked, eyeing the map thoughtfully. "I'm not certain confrontation is the safest option."

"Oh, come now," Emma said gently. "Sometimes, you need to face these things head-on. Besides, we'll all be there to support Catherine."

As the day wore on, the plan grew more refined. Julie was tasked with creating a series of subtle signals they could use to communicate without alerting Richard.

Lisa, ever the voice of reason, was put in charge of the "coordination centre" (which was Rosie's kitchen, now filled with mobile phones and an unnecessarily large amount of snacks).

Trisha, drawing on her experience in event planning, coordinated the logistics with admirable precision.

"Right," she said, consulting her notebook. "Emma, you'll be stationed here at the café-"

As evening approached, they put the final touches to their plan.

Catherine, looking both nervous and determined, was dressed for her "outing" - an elaborate ruse involving Mike (who had been roped into the scheme with surprisingly little persuasion) and Chez Katarine, the new French bistro in town.

"Remember," Trisha instructed as they did a final run-through, "the signal is two taps on your water glass. If you spot Richard, you give the signal, and we'll move into position."

Catherine nodded solemnly. "Got it. Two taps. Though I'm a bit worried I might get nervous and accidentally set you all off if I'm enjoying my wine."

As darkness fell, Operation Closure swung into action. Rosie found herself seated at a corner table in the bistro, menu in hand but eyes scanning the room. She felt a mix of anticipation and nervousness, but also a sense of purpose.

Who would have thought that at her age, she'd be involved in such a delicate intervention?

"Eagle One to Mama Bear," Emma's voice came softly through the phone. "The Cheese has entered the building. I repeat, the Cheese has entered the building."

Rosie rolled her eyes fondly. "Emma, we agreed you'd be Rosebud, I'd be Sunflower, and Catherine would be Bluebell. Try to stick to the script."

"Well, excuse me for trying to inject a little excitement into our operation," Emma replied, a smile evident in her voice. "Fine. Rosebud to Sunflower. Bluebell is seated. Over."

For the next hour, Rosie and her friends maintained their

positions, watching as Catherine and Mike enjoyed their meal. The atmosphere was tense but controlled, each woman ready to play her part if needed.

Just as Rosie was beginning to think their plan might have been unnecessary, she spotted a familiar figure entering the bistro. Richard, looking uncomfortable and out of place, was making his way towards Catherine's table.

"This is not a drill," Rosie murmured into her phone. "The subject has entered the building. I repeat, the subject has entered the building."

What followed was a scene of carefully orchestrated intervention.

Emma smoothly intercepted Richard before he could reach Catherine's table, engaging him in conversation with a mix of charm and firm resolve.

Julie and Lisa moved to flank Catherine, offering silent support as Mike discreetly stepped aside, but hovered incase things became difficult.

Trisha, ever the professional, coordinated their movements with subtle gestures, ensuring that Richard was gently but firmly guided to a quiet corner of the bistro where they could talk privately. Rosie, watching from her position at the corner table, felt a surge of pride in her friends.

This was not how she'd envisioned spending her golden years, but she had to admit, it was far more meaningful than she could have imagined.

The confrontation, when it came, was both emotional and cathartic.

Catherine, supported by her friends, spoke to Richard with a clarity and strength that seemed to take him by surprise. She could see him looking around the packed bistro nervously, aware that everyone was watching them.

Catherine laid out her feelings, her frustrations, and her firm desire for him to respect her boundaries and move on.

Richard, faced with the united front of the women and the quiet dignity of Catherine's words, seemed to deflate.

The bravado and denial that had fuelled his behaviour crumbled away, leaving a man who looked lost and, finally, ashamed.

As the evening drew to a close, with Richard agreeing to seek counselling and respect Catherine's wishes, Rosie looked around at her friends.

They were a sight to behold - Emma radiating quiet triumph, Julie sketching the scene with swift, emotive strokes, Lisa offering comforting words to a tearful but relieved Catherine, and Trisha coordinating with the bistro staff to thank them for their help.

"FACING THE FUTURE"

*R*osie stood in her bedroom, looking into her jewellery box and frowning at its contents as if they had personally offended her.

What jewellery should one wear to discuss a thirty-year marriage? And what clothes? She had briefly considered her leopard print blouse – a symbol of her newfound freedom – but decided that might be a tad insensitive.

Finally, she settled on a simple blue dress that Derek had always liked. A peace offering of sorts. Now she needed the right earrings to wear with it...earrings that said 'I like and respect you enough to make an effort, but I am not in any way flirting with you.'

The drive to the mediator's office was difficult. With each mile, Rosie's mind raced with memories – her wedding day, bringing Mary home from the hospital, family holidays, quiet evenings at home. But alongside these happy recollections came others: the arguments, the growing distance, the feeling of invisibility that had plagued her in the last years of their marriage.

As she pulled into the car park, she spotted Derek's car

already there. Always punctual, that was Derek. She took a deep breath, squared her shoulders, and stepped out of the car.

"You can do this, Rosie," she muttered to herself. "You faced down Richard. This is a piece of cake."

She found Derek in the waiting room, looking as nervous as she felt. He stood when he saw her, a tentative smile on his face. "Rosie," he said, his voice warm. "You look lovely."

"Thank you," she replied, suddenly feeling shy. "You look well too."

An awkward moment passed as they both hesitated, as they always did, unsure whether to hug, shake hands, or simply nod politely.

They were saved from their indecision by the arrival of Mrs Pemberton, a sturdy woman who looked like she had been born in a tweed suit and had possibly never smiled in her life.

"Mr. and Mrs. Brown," she intoned, "if you'll follow me."

As they settled into the overstuffed leather chairs in Mrs. Pemberton's office, Rosie felt like she had been called in to see the headmistress and was about to be scolded for some unknown transgression. She half expected Mrs Pemberton to pull out a cane and demand lines.

"Now," Mrs Pemberton began. "We are here to discuss your relationship." And so began the most surreal experience Rosie had ever encountered. Sitting across from Derek, with the mediator's gentle guidance, they began to unpack thirty years of shared life.

Memories, both joyous and painful, were laid bare like delicate china, each to be examined and carefully considered. Mrs Pemberton insisted on them calling her Sarah, and revealed herself to be a much kinder, gentler person than they had first imagined.

BERNICE BLOOM

As soon as the conversation became tricky, she'd smile warmly: "Let's talk about what brought you both here today."

Derek leaned forward, his eyes earnest. "I want to save our marriage," he said, his voice thick with emotion. "Rosie, I know I've made mistakes, but I believe we can work through this. We've built a life together, and I'm not ready to let that go."

Rosie felt a lump form in her throat. She could see the hope in Derek's eyes, the genuine desire to mend what was broken. But alongside that recognition came a whisper of doubt, a question she couldn't quite silence: Was wanting to save their marriage enough?

"Derek," she began slowly, choosing her words with care, "I appreciate that you want to try. But I'm not sure if I'm in the same place. These past few years apart... they've shown me a different side of life, of myself."

Sarah nodded encouragingly. "It's important to be honest about your feelings, Rosie. Can you elaborate on what you've discovered about yourself?"

Rosie took a deep breath, her mind flashing to impromptu adventures with the Sensational Sixties Squad, to newfound confidence, to laughter-filled evenings that didn't revolve around a shared routine.

"I've found a sense of independence I didn't know I was missing," she admitted. "I've rediscovered parts of myself that I thought were long gone."

Derek's face fell, but he nodded slowly. "I understand," he said softly. "I've noticed the change in you, Rosie. You seem... lighter, somehow. Happier."

The rest of the session passed in a blur of gentle questions and careful answers. They discussed their history, their present, and tentatively, their future.

Derek spoke of his regrets, of his desire to rebuild. Rosie listened and tried to respond in the kindest way she could, but the bottom line was that she didn't think there was anything left to rebuild. She resisted the urgent to bring up the affair. She talked about them now: two people who had simply grown apart.

As they left the mediator's office, Rosie felt emotionally drained but oddly peaceful. They had agreed to take things slowly, to continue with the mediation process without making any firm decisions yet.

"Rosie," Derek said as they reached their cars, "thank you for being willing to try. Whatever happens... I want you to be happy."

Rosie felt a rush of affection for this man who had been her partner for so long. "Thank you, Derek," she replied softly. "I want that for you, too."

As she drove home, Rosie's mind whirled with thoughts and emotions. She barely noticed the journey, finding herself in her driveway without any real memory of the drive. As if summoned by her tumultuous thoughts, her phone buzzed with a series of messages.

Emma: "Well? How did it go? Do I need to bring the emergency chocolate?"

Lisa: "Thinking of you, Rosie. Here if you need to talk."

Julie: "Just finished a painting I'm calling 'Crossroads'. Want to see it?"

Catherine: "Sending hugs and a virtual pot of tea. The real thing is waiting whenever you're ready."

Trisha: "Remember, whatever you decide, we're here for you. Also, I've got cake."

Rosie smiled. Those women knew exactly what to say to cheer her up.

Her phone bleeped again with a message from Emma. "We're all at mine if you fancy coming round. No pressure, but we're here when you need us."

Rosie turned the key in the ignition, reversed off her

drive, and headed straight for her friend's house. Emma opened the door before Rosie could even knock.

"There you are," she said softly, pulling Rosie into a warm hug. "Come in, love. We've got tea, and biscuits, and Julie's brought her latest masterpiece. It's... well, you'll see."

Rosie found herself ushered into Emma's living room, which had been transformed into a cosy haven of support. Catherine was brewing a pot of tea. Julie was quietly explaining her new painting – a swirling mass of paths and colours that did indeed seem to capture the essence of being at a crossroads. Trisha, true to her word, had brought cake. Lisa was arranging a tempting array of biscuits on the coffee table.

"I wasn't sure what flavour best said 'supportive regardless of your decision', so I got a selection," she explained.

As Rosie sank onto the sofa, feeling enveloped by the love and support surrounding her, Emma pressed a steaming mug of tea into her hands.

"Right," she said gently, settling in beside Rosie. "Whenever you're ready to talk, we're here to listen. No pressure, no judgement."

Rosie felt tears prick at her eyes, overwhelmed by the kindness of her friends. "Thank you," she managed, taking a sip of tea to steady herself. "It was... intense. Derek wants to try to save the marriage."

A ripple of understanding passed through the group. "And how do you feel about that?" Lisa asked softly, her eyes full of compassion.

Rosie sighed, cradling her mug. "I'm not sure," she admitted. "Part of me remembers the good times, the life we built together. But another part..."

"Wants to see where this new chapter might lead?" Catherine finished gently.

Rosie nodded, feeling a mix of guilt and relief at having her feelings understood. "Is that selfish of me?"

"Not at all," Trisha said firmly. "You're allowed to prioritise your happiness, Rosie. It's not selfish to want to explore this new side of yourself."

As her friends offered words of support and encouragement, Rosie felt the knot of tension in her chest begin to loosen. They didn't push her towards any particular decision and didn't judge her for her uncertainty. They simply listened, offered comfort, and reminded her of her strength.

"You know," Julie mused, looking thoughtfully at her painting, "life rarely gives us clear-cut paths. Sometimes we have to forge our way."

"THE LAST HURRAH"

Rosie stood in the middle of her living room, surveying the chaos around her with a mixture of amusement and mild horror. Streamers hung from every available surface, balloons bobbed gently against the ceiling, and a banner proclaiming: "Goodbye House, Hello Adventure!" stretched across the fireplace.

The banner, lovingly crafted by Julie, featured what appeared to be a house with legs running towards a sunset made entirely of glitter.

"Remind me again why I thought this was a good idea?" Rosie muttered to herself as she adjusted a slightly lopsided flower arrangement.

"Because, darling," Emma's voice rang out as she swept into the room carrying what looked suspiciously like a punch bowl, "you can't leave this house without giving it a proper send-off. Now, where shall we put the libations?"

Rosie eyed the punch bowl warily. "Emma, please tell me that's not your infamous 'Sensational Sixty' cocktail. I still haven't recovered from the last time."

Emma's eyes twinkled mischievously. "Of course not!

This is my new creation – 'The House Warmer.' Or should that be 'House Cooler' since we're leaving? Either way, I promise it's only slightly lethal."

Before Rosie could protest, the doorbell rang. She opened it to find Lisa on the doorstep, looking uncharacteristically flustered and carrying an enormous cake box. "Rosie, thank goodness," Lisa said, bustling past her. "You won't believe what happened. The bakery mixed up our order. Instead of 'Farewell to Rosie's House,' the cake says 'Congratulations on Your Vasectomy, Ross'."

Rosie blinked, trying to process this information. "I... what?"

Lisa set the box down on the dining table, lifting the lid to reveal a truly impressive cake adorned with anatomically correct decorations that Rosie decided she'd rather not examine too closely.

"I tried to explain the mistake, but the baker just kept insisting that this was the only cake they had there."

Emma, who had wandered over to inspect the cake, burst into laughter. "Oh, this is perfect! Nothing says 'new beginnings' quite like celebrating the end of someone else's fertility. Ross, whoever he is, will just have to find another cake."

As Rosie and Lisa debated the merits of trying to scrape off the more questionable decorations, the house gradually filled with guests.

Julie arrived with an easel and art supplies, declaring her intention to create a "living memory" of the party. Catherine brought enough food to feed a small army, explaining that she wasn't sure what kind of snacks were appropriate for a "house funeral."

Trisha, ever the organiser, had taken it upon herself to create a schedule for the evening. "I've allotted time for mingling, reminiscing, and a brief period for Emma to teach everyone the dance routine she's been threatening us with," she explained, brandishing a colour-coded chart.

"Dance routine?" Rosie asked weakly, but her question was drowned out by the arrival of more guests. Soon, the house was buzzing with conversation and laughter. Neighbours Rosie had known for years mingled with newer friends, all sharing stories and memories of the house that had been Rosie's home for so long.

Mrs Fitzgerald from next door cornered Rosie by the punch bowl, her eyes slightly glazed from Emma's concoction. "I'll never forget the time your cat got stuck in our chimney," she reminisced. "Took three firemen and a very confused pizza delivery boy to get him out!"

Rosie nodded politely, trying to remember if she'd ever owned a cat. She made a mental note to cut Mrs Fitzgerald off from the punch.

The evening wore on and Rosie found herself swept up in a whirlwind of emotions. Every room held a memory – some joyful, some bittersweet.

In the kitchen, she remembered teaching Mary to bake cookies, flour covering every surface and giggles filling the air. In the study, she recalled long nights working, fuelled by tea and determination.

She was lost in thought, staring at a family photo on the mantelpiece, when a familiar voice made her heart skip a beat. "Penny for your thoughts?" Rosie turned to find Mike standing behind her, a warm smile on his face and a bottle of wine in his hand.

"Mike! You came," she said, unable to keep the pleasure out of her voice.

"Wouldn't miss it for the world," he replied. "Though I have to admit, I'm a little concerned about the cake. Is there something you haven't told me about a 'Ross' in your life?"

Rosie laughed, feeling some of the melancholy of the

evening lift. "Oh, that. It's a long story involving a mix-up at the bakery and possibly the end of someone's genetic line. But never mind that – I'm so glad you're here."

As they chatted, Emma's voice came thundering through the room, amplified by what appeared to be a megaphone fashioned out of a wine bottle and a rolled-up magazine. "Ladies and gentlemen, and those who are fabulously neither," she announced, "it's time for the main event of the evening – the House Memory Tour!"

A chorus of cheers (and a few confused murmurs from those who hadn't been warned about Emma's penchant for impromptu events) filled the air.

"Now," Emma continued, somehow managing to look both regal and slightly unsteady as she climbed onto a chair, "we'll be going room by room, sharing our favourite memories of Rosie's house. And for each memory shared, we'll raise a toast! Don't worry, I've prepared non-alcoholic options for the lightweights among us." She winked at Lisa, who rolled her eyes good-naturedly.

What followed was a meandering, slightly chaotic, but ultimately heartwarming journey through Rosie's home. In the kitchen, Mary (who had arrived fashionably late with the twins in tow) recounted the time she'd tried to surprise Rosie with breakfast in bed, resulting in a small fire and the discovery that pancake batter could defy gravity if applied with enough enthusiasm to the ceiling.

In the living room, Catherine shared the story of their sleepover, after Rosie had gone on her first date with Mike.

As they moved upstairs, Julie insisted on recreating the infamous "Yoga Incident" in Rosie's bedroom, nearly taking out a lamp and two unsuspecting guests in her enthusiastic demonstration of a "downward-facing disaster."

Each story, each memory shared, felt like a thread weaving together the tapestry of Rosie's life in this house.

There were tears, as Rosie and Mary hugged, and there was laughter – particularly when Emma recounted the time she'd tried to install a disco ball in the guest room as a "surprise home improvement."

Through it all, Rosie felt Mike's steady presence beside her, his hand occasionally finding hers in quiet support. She caught him more than once looking at her with an expression that made her heart flutter in a most unseemly (but not unwelcome) way for a woman of her age.

As the tour wound down, ending back in the living room, Emma called for silence. "And now," she said, her voice taking on a theatrical solemnity, "it's time for the lady of the house herself to share a memory.

Rosie, darling, the floor is yours."

All eyes turned to Rosie. She felt a moment of panic – how could she possibly sum up thirty years of life in this house in one memory? But as she looked around at the faces of her friends, old and new, she knew exactly what to say.

"My favourite memory of this house," she began, her voice strong despite the lump in her throat, "is happening right now. This house has been a home not just because of the memories it holds, but because of the people who have filled it with love and laughter. Yes, even you, Emma, with your glitter-based solutions to life's problems."

A ripple of affectionate laughter went through the room. "I thought selling this house would be an ending," Rosie continued. "But being here with all of you tonight, I realise it's just the beginning of a new adventure. So thank you – for the memories we've shared, and for the ones we've yet to make."

There was a moment of silence as her words sank in, broken only by the sound of Catherine blowing her nose loudly into what appeared to be one of Julie's paintbrushes.

Then Emma, never one to let a moment become too

sentimental, raised her glass high. "To Rosie!" she declared. "May our next home be filled with as much love, laughter, and impromptu dance parties as this one!"

"To Rosie!" the room echoed, glasses clinking and voices raised in a cacophony of affection.

As the party resumed its cheerful chaos around her, Rosie found herself by the window, looking out at the garden where she'd spent so many peaceful mornings. She felt rather than heard Mike approach.

"You okay?" he asked softly. Rosie nodded, smiling up at him. "You know, I am. It's bittersweet, of course, but... I'm excited for what comes next."

Mike's hand found hers, their fingers intertwining naturally.

"I'm excited too," he said. "Especially if it involves more parties like this. Hopefully without such creatively iced cakes."

Rosie laughed, leaning into him slightly. "Oh, I don't know. I think the Sensational Sixties Squad Headquarters might need a mascot. Why not a vasectomy cake?"

Their moment was interrupted by a crash from the kitchen, followed by Emma's voice floating out: "Nobody panic! The punch bowl is safe. Can't say the same for Rosie's fine china, but really, who needs plates when you're starting a new adventure?"

Rosie sighed, but couldn't keep the fondness out of her voice as she said, "I should probably go see what's broken. Coming?"

Mike grinned, squeezing her hand and they made their way to the kitchen, navigating through guests who were now engaged in what appeared to be a very competitive game of charades (Julie was currently trying to act out "Fifty Shades of Grey" using only a feather duster and a very confused looking houseplant).

The kitchen was a scene of cheerful disaster. Emma, covered in what Rosie hoped was just punch, was attempting to sweep up shards of her best serving platter while simultaneously arguing with Lisa about the merits of using a salad bowl as an emergency punch container.

"It's the perfect solution!" Emma insisted. "It's big, it's deep, and let's be honest, nobody was going to eat salad at this shindig anyway."

Lisa, looking torn between exasperation and amusement, caught sight of Rosie and Mike.

"Oh, thank goodness," she said. "Rosie, please tell Emma that we can't serve punch out of your salad bowl. It's... uncultured."

Emma scoffed. "Uncultured? Lisa, darling, I'm glad we didn't know each other when I was younger and drinking cheap wine out of shoes."

Rosie held up her hands in mock surrender. "Far be it from me to get between Emma and her mission to serve alcohol from increasingly inappropriate containers. Use the salad bowl if you must, but please, for the love of all that's holy, wash it first."

As Emma crowed in triumph and Lisa muttered something about investing in spare pun bowls for future gatherings, Rosie turned to survey the rest of the kitchen. It was a mess, to be sure – dishes piled in the sink, half-empty glasses littering every surface, and what appeared to be the remnants of Catherine's attempt at flambéing something (despite the distinct lack of a proper flambé dish or, indeed, any culinary skill whatsoever).

But it was a happy mess. A mess full of life and laughter and friendship.

Looking at it, Rosie suddenly realized that this – this joyful chaos – was what she'd been missing in the latter years of her marriage. This sense of adventure, of never quite knowing what might happen next but being excited to find out.

She turned to Mike, who had been watching the scene with an amused smile. "I'm glad you're here," she said, "I like it when you're here."

Mike's smile widened. "Well, that's lucky because I like being here," he replied, leaning in to plant a soft kiss on her cheek. Of course, this tender moment was immediately interrupted by a shout from the living room.

"Oi, lovebirds!" Emma's voice rang out. "Stop canoodling in the kitchen and get in here! Julie's about to unveil her masterpiece, and I've got twenty quid riding on it being either a nude portrait of the house or an interpretive piece about divorce featuring at least three different bodily fluids as paint!"

Rosie and Mike exchanged a look – part exasperation, part amusement.

"Shall we?" Mike asked, offering his arm with exaggerated gallantry.

Rosie laughed, linking her arm through his. "Oh, why not? I have a feeling we're about to witness either an artistic triumph or a crime against canvas. Either way, it'll be memorable."

As they made their way back to the living room, Rosie took one last look around her kitchen. Yes, she was leaving this house. But she wasn't leaving behind the warmth, the laughter, or the love that had filled it. She was taking all of that with her, into whatever adventure came next.

The living room had been transformed into an impromptu art gallery, with Julie's easel taking centre stage. A sheet covered what Rosie assumed was the painting, adding an air of dramatic mystery to the proceedings.

"Ladies and gentlemen," Julie announced, her voice carrying the gravitas of a museum curator unveiling a long-lost masterpiece, "I present to you: 'Rosie's House: A Journey Through Time and Questionable Fashion Choices'!"

With a flourish that would have made any magician proud, Julie whipped off the sheet. There was a moment of stunned silence as the gathered guests tried to make sense of what they were seeing. The painting was... well, it was certainly something. At its centre was a fairly accurate rendition of Rosie's house, but surrounding it were swirls of colour and what appeared to be scenes from various moments in Rosie's life. There was a remarkably detailed depiction of the "Yoga Incident," complete with Catherine frozen in an impossible pose and Emma wielding what looked suspiciously like a wine bottle instead of a yoga mat. In one corner, Rosie spotted what she assumed was meant to be her first meeting with the Sensational Sixties Squad, though why Julie had chosen to paint them all wearing superhero capes was anyone's guess.

"It's... certainly unique," Lisa offered diplomatically.

"It's bloody brilliant is what it is!" Emma declared, already halfway to tipsy and loving every bizarre inch of the canvas. "Look, she's even included that time we tried to give Rosie a makeover."

Rosie, torn between mortification and amusement, stepped closer to examine the painting. Despite its eccentricities (or perhaps because of them), she found herself deeply touched. Every strange little scene represented a moment of friendship, of laughter, of life lived to the fullest.

"Julie," she said, her voice thick with emotion, "it's perfect. It's us."

Julie beamed, clearly pleased with the reception. "I wanted to capture not just the house, but the spirit of everything that's happened here. All the joy, the craziness, the love that has happened since we all met."

"Well, she's certainly captured the craziness," Mike murmured in Rosie's ear, causing her to stifle a giggle.

As the guests gathered around to examine the painting more closely, exclaiming over various details and sharing the stories behind them, Rosie felt a sense of completion wash over her.

This was the perfect way to say goodbye to her home – surrounded by friends, laughter, and a truly bizarre piece of art that somehow encapsulated it all.

The party continued late into the night, fuelled by Emma's punch (now served from the salad bowl, much to Lisa's ongoing dismay) and a seemingly endless supply of stories and laughter.

By the time the last guest had been poured into a taxi, the house looked like it had hosted a particularly enthusiastic tornado.

Rosie stood in the doorway, surveying the aftermath with a mix of exhaustion and contentment. Streamers hung limply from the ceiling, deflated balloons littered the floor, and Julie's masterpiece stood proudly (if slightly askew) in the corner, a testament to the evening's festivities.

"Well," Mike said, coming up behind her and wrapping an arm around her waist, "I'd say that was a successful send-off."

Rosie leaned into him, grateful for his steady presence.

"It certainly was. Though I'm not sure my poor house will ever recover."

"Oh, pish posh," Emma's voice floated in from the living room, where she was attempting to untangle herself from a string of fairy lights. "Houses are meant to be lived in, not preserved like museums. And I'd say we gave this one a proper send-off, wouldn't you?"

Lisa, who was methodically sorting recyclables from general waste (because even in the aftermath of a party, some habits die hard), nodded in agreement. "It was a lovely evening, Rosie. However, I do think we should ban Emma from punch-making duties for the foreseeable future. I'm fairly certain I saw Mary trying to salsa with your coat rack at one point."

"That wasn't the punch," Julie chimed in, carefully wrapping her painting for transport. "That was just Mary being Mary."

As they continued to tidy up, sharing quiet laughs and gentle reminiscences, Rosie felt a profound sense of gratitude wash over her.

"You know," Trisha said, pausing in her meticulous note-taking of gift-givers (because heaven forbid anyone should go unthanked), "I think this party was the perfect preview of what life in the Sensational Sixties Squad Headquarters will be like."

Catherine, who was half-asleep on the sofa, roused herself enough to ask, "You mean chaotic, slightly ridiculous, and fuelled by Emma's questionable cocktails?"

"Exactly!" Emma said triumphantly. "It's going to be marvellous."

As the first light of dawn began to peek through the windows, Rosie found herself alone in the kitchen. The others had finally been persuaded to go home (or in Emma's case, to take a nap in the bathtub, as she insisted she was "too comfortable to move").

Mike had left reluctantly, but not before extracting a promise of dinner later in the week.

Rosie ran her hand along the familiar countertop, remembering all the meals prepared here, all the late-night cups of tea, all the moments big and small that had made up her life in this house.

She thought she might cry, but instead found herself smiling.

"Thank you," she whispered to the empty room. "For everything."

Just then, a crash from the living room, followed by Emma's muffled voice calling out, "I'm okay! The lamp's not, but I'm fine!", broke the moment. Rosie laughed, shaking her head fondly.

As she went to rescue Emma, Rosie felt a sense of excitement bubbling up inside her. They were all going to live together in a huge house.

They were going to be like the Golden Girls. All they had to do now was to work out how organise the place and decorate it to everyone's tastes…

"NEW BEGINNINGS"

Rosie stood in the middle of her now-empty living room, the echo of her footsteps a stark reminder of how quickly a house becomes just a building once you start removing the life from it.

She clutched a manila envelope containing the finalised papers for the purchase of their new shared home, feeling as though she were holding the key to her future.

"Well," she said to the bare walls, "I suppose this is it, then."

As if on cue, the front door opened, and Emma's voice rang out, "Darling! Are you ready for the next chapter of our grand adventure?"

Before Rosie could respond, the rest of the Sensational Sixties Squad filed in behind Emma.

Lisa, ever practical, was carrying a folder full of renovation ideas.

Julie had her sketchpad tucked under one arm and a determined glint in her eye that suggested she was already planning to document their new home in paint.

Catherine was laden down with what looked like enough snacks to fuel their brainstorming session, while Trisha brought up the rear with a stack of interior design magazines.

"Emma," Rosie said, smiling warmly, "I can't believe we're doing this. Are we mad?"

Emma's eyes twinkled with mischief. "Darling, the best people usually are. Now, shall we head off to our new palace and start planning how to turn it into a home fit for five fabulous women?"

Rosie laughed. Trust Emma to turn house renovation into an exciting escapade.

"Well, I appreciate the enthusiasm, but I'm not sure the world is ready for our particular brand of... creativity."

"Nonsense!" Emma declared. "They'll be so impressed by our impeccable taste that they'll be begging us to start our own home makeover show."

"Right," Trisha interjected, clearly deciding it was time to bring some order to the proceedings. "I've brought some magazines for inspiration, and I've made a list of local interior designers we might want to consult."

"Ooh, let me see!" Catherine exclaimed, peering over Trisha's shoulder at the magazines. "Oh, I like that colour scheme. It reminds me of that lovely bed and breakfast we stayed at in the Cotswolds."

"Ladies," Rosie said, her voice soft with emotion, "I just want to say thank you. For everything. For being here, for this mad idea of living together, for... well, for being you."

Lisa laid a comforting hand on Rosie's arm. "Oh, Rosie. We wouldn't have it any other way. Just think of all the fun we'll have, and the support we can give each other."

"Plus," Julie added, "think of the artistic possibilities! I can already envision a series of paintings: 'The Golden Girls' New Adventure' or maybe 'Sixties and Sensational: A Study in Shared Living and Joy.'"

As they made their way to their new home, the conversation in the car was a delightful mix of practical considerations and flights of fancy. Emma was adamant that they needed a "fabulous entertaining space for our soirées, darling," while Lisa was more concerned with ensuring the house was energy-efficient and easy to maintain.

When they pulled up to the sprawling country house that was to be their new home, Rosie felt a flutter of excitement in her chest. The red brick facade and the wild, rambling garden held so much potential.

"Oh," Rosie breathed, taking it all in. "Oh, it's even more beautiful than I remembered."

As they wandered through the rooms, each woman's personality began to shine through in their ideas for the space. Julie was enchanted by the light in what would become her studio, already planning where to set up her easel.

Catherine was examining the kitchen with a critical eye, muttering about the need for more counter space for her baking experiments.

Emma, true to form, was most excited about the grand living room. "Just imagine, darlings," she said, gesturing expansively, "cocktail parties, book club meetings, impromptu dance sessions – all right here!"

Lisa, meanwhile, was making notes about necessary repairs and upgrades. "We'll need to check the wiring," she mused, "and perhaps consider solar panels for the roof."

As they gathered in what would soon be their shared living room, Rosie felt a warmth spread through her.

"Right," Trisha said, pulling out a notebook. "Shall we start making some concrete plans? I think we should tackle one room at a time, starting with the communal spaces."

What followed was a lively discussion filled with laughter, gentle disagreements, and moments of pure inspiration. Emma's grand visions were tempered by Lisa's practicality, while Julie's artistic ideas were balanced by Catherine's focus on comfort and functionality.

As the afternoon wore on, fuelled by Catherine's snacks and the occasional cup of tea, their plans began to take shape. The house, which had seemed almost overwhelmingly large at first, now felt full of possibility.

"You know," Rosie said during a lull in the conversation, "a year ago, I never could have imagined this. Living with my best friends, starting a whole new chapter at our age."

"Oh, darling," Emma said, giving her a gentle squeeze, "age is just a number. We're not getting older, we're getting better. Like a fine wine or a well-aged cheese."

"Or like Emma's jokes," Catherine quipped. "They don't improve with age, but we've grown fond of them anyway."

The future stretched out before them, not as a well-worn path, but as an open road full of potential. It was exciting. It was terrifying. It was exactly what they all needed. Because life, Rosie was learning, didn't end at sixty. It just got more interesting.

As the sun began to set, casting a warm glow through the windows of their new home, the Sensational Sixties Squad raised their teacups in a toast.

"To new beginnings," Rosie said.

"To adventures yet to come," Lisa added.

"To midnight feasts and morning yoga," Catherine chimed in.

"To art in all its forms," Julie declared.

"To making this house a home," Trisha said softly.

"And to us," Emma finished with a flourish. "May we always be sensational, no matter what age we are!"

As they clinked their cups together.

Rosie just smiled. This was a life full of possibility, friendship, and the promise of new adventures.

And really, what more could a woman ask for in her golden years?

WANT to know how the women get on in their shared house?
See Sassy Sisterhood
UK: My Book
US: My Book

SASSY SISTERHOOD

SIX WOMEN: ONE HOUSE: TONNES OF PARTYING AND LOTS OF GENTLEMEN CALLERS.

But the twist is that these women are not 20. They're all over 60 and determined to stay young and adventurous and enjoy life like they did when they were young

"This is like GOLDEN GIRLS for the new millennium."

ROSIE BROWN *and her band of merry 60-somethings have decided to move in together. What could go wrong? It'll be like a modern version of Golden Girls, surely?*

The problem is that these women come with a whole pile of history and a determination to throw caution to the wind.

*There's **Rosie** who is dating a handsome doctor while her estranged husband is desperate to get her back. Her daughter, Mary (star of the Mary Brown series of books) is torn - she'd love her parents to get back together but thinks the hunky doctor is lovely and good for her mum. Which way will Rosie go? Back to a past she knows, or forward into adventure and the unknown?*

***Emma**, the party girl, is dead-set on partying every night, and will not take no for an answer.*

***Lisa** is having an affair with a famous actor whom the others aren't keen on. They are forced to endure the dull plays he 'stars in'* *and long for her to find someone more down to earth and less 'actor-y'.*

Julie *is having a huge breakthrough as an artist, meaning a small art gallery being established in their home, and a plethora of sophisticated guests coming to visit. How will Lord and Lady Van de Hay feel about a young man emerging from **Maria**'s room, dishevelled and half-dressed? And how will Maris's estranged husband, David, react?*

*And what will happen when David teams up with **Catherine**'s ex, Richard, to try and disrupt the women and cause them as many problems as possible?*

But all of that pales into insignificance when Lisa is taken seriously ill.

"THIS IS A GREAT NEW SERIES. **Whether you're 18, or 80, you will love its anarchic style with a heart of pure gold.**"

"**I love these books. WHY IS THERE NOT A FILM SERIES!!**""**A heartwarming tale that proves it's never too late to rewrite your story - even if you need reading glasses to see the page.**"

So grab your most outrageous hat, pour yourself a cheeky glass of sherry, and get ready to join Rosie on the adventure of a lifetime!

Warning: *This book may cause spontaneous laughter, uncontrollable urges to tango, and a sudden desire to dazzle your walking stick. Reader discretion is advised!*

Printed in Great Britain
by Amazon